Living in the Light

Lessons and Tools for
Your Spiritual Journey

By: Susan Duncan

iUniverse, Inc.
New York   Bloomington

iUniverse books may be ordered through booksellers or by contacting:

iUniverse
1663 Liberty Drive
Bloomington, IN 47403
www.iuniverse.com
1-800-Authors (1-800-288-4677)

Because of the dynamic nature of the Internet, any Web addresses or links
contained in this book may have changed since publication and may no longer be
valid. The views expressed in this work are solely those of the author and do not
necessarily reflect the views of the publisher, and the publisher hereby disclaims
any responsibility for them.

ISBN: 978-1-4401-6568-9 (sc)
ISBN: 978-1-4401-6569-6 (ebook)
ISBN: 978-1-4401-6570-2 (hc)

Printed in the United States of America

iUniverse rev. date: 9/9/2009

Dedication

To my mother, Doris, who supports me in all of my life projects; to my grandmother, Golden, who taught me how to write the alphabet and so much more; and gratefully to all of the readers of my newsletter, **_Living In The Light_**.

Contents

30 "IN-LIGHTENED" THINGS TO DO

AFFIRMATIONS

Introduction

In May 1997, I published my first newsletter titled "Living In The Light." I was committed to developing two business ventures that I had undertaken. I sold herbal products and taught about the uses and benefits of herbs and vitamins. I also wanted to alert people about the healing properties of crystals and gemstones, and sell my handcrafted crystal jewelry. I desired a vehicle to share in-depth information about these products and stones. I felt that the newsletter would also serve as a marketing tool for my business.

At the beginning of each newsletter, I would write a personal message to my readers – a spiritually conscious message. I titled this section "Message From Susan." It required no research because it was written from my heart and soul. It was the part that could be either the hardest or easiest to write. After prayer and meditation, many times I would receive the entire message without thinking or engaging my brain. I consciously provided a pen, and I could not seem to write the information down fast enough. Sometimes I would have written the entire newsletter, and then prayed and waited for an idea for the opening message.

Through the years, I received tremendous positive response from my newsletter readers. This has served as a blessing to me. As I initially desired, my businesses have grown over the years. However, I have received the most enthusiastic feedback from the

"Message From Susan" section. Readers continually called and told me how various topics I address help them with their life situations and challenges. Some said that it seemed as though I was speaking directly to them and what they were currently experiencing. This response always inspired me to keep writing. I am eternally grateful to God and to each reader of the newsletter for allowing me to fulfill my purpose.

Many readers have asked me to put the ideas into book form. A book titled *Living in the Light* simmered in my mind and heart for some time. After eleven years of writing the newsletter, it finally seemed to be the right moment. After I began creating the book, I recalled that in numerology, eleven is a spiritual number and denotes "light." The numerical value for the letters in the word "light" adds up to eleven. I thought maybe this truly is the proper time to write the book, *Living in the Light.*

This book consists of essays on various spiritual topics that can be applied to most people's lives. In addition, I have added a "to-do" list of spiritually conscious things to do; and a list of affirmations that can be spoken in order to create and affirm positive conditions in your life.

In addition to my personal experiences over the years, I have studied numerous religious, spiritual, and metaphysical practices and principles including Christianity and the New Thought religions. This book discusses many of the spiritual lessons I have learned, and am still learning, over my years of trying to find the most peaceful, loving, joyful, and prosperous way to live. It puts forth my observations as I continually attempt to travel the path of spiritual growth. I can honestly say that I am in a better place now than I was when I started the newsletter eleven years ago. My experiences, observations, and challenges during this time have helped me to grow spiritually, although I see myself on a continuous journey of learning throughout this lifetime. Hopefully, and prayerfully, I will continue to pay attention to all the signs and continue to learn.

It is my hope that some chapter, paragraph, or phrase within this book will assist others as they travel their spiritual paths. We are all journeying together. Perhaps something in the book will speak to some specific life challenge that you are facing. As you read, take the information in, and allow it to vibrate within you. If the information feels right and resonates with your spirit, keep that information. As you read, I send you light and love, as we are all One.

The Essays

Chapter 1
Progress Along Your Spiritual Path May Not Be A Straight Line

Have you ever felt that you had overcome some undesirable trait in your personality, or an unwanted habit, only to find that it shows up later on in your life? For example, perhaps you are someone who is self-centered, and you do not like to share. For years, you may have tried to change this trait and, in your opinion, you had succeeded. You feel that you have become more generous with those around you. But, just when you thought you had mastered the art of "giving," along comes some situation where you may really hate to share with others. It may not be as obvious as sharing the last piece of pie at the dinner table. It may be as subtle as not wanting to share praise given for a successful work project that you accomplished with a deserving fellow colleague.

Usually when we are on our paths to spiritual development, we take stock of ourselves and analyze our feelings and our actions from time to time during our journey. This, of course, needs to be done so that we know whether we should change directions in order to make our lives and ourselves better—ultimately arriving at our desired spiritual destination. Once we decide upon the traits that we want to change, we may use many tools to assist this change, such as prayer, affirmations, meditation, and spiritual readings. All of these tools help us develop positive traits within ourselves that are more reflective of the way God, the Creator, lives through us.

In time, after traveling along this spiritual path, we may feel that we have overcome whatever trait we identified as undesirable in our lives. We may even feel like transformed individuals. Some of us may even feel a little smug and "better than" as a result of our assumed transformation.

Time continues to elapse and it really is sometimes depressing when we see this very trait that we have removed from our being pop up again. And it is even more perplexing when it comes back in a subtle form, which sometimes makes it difficult to recognize that it is the same old trait. We wonder, "How can it be showing up again? How can we be doing or feeling this same thing again?"

I have actually experienced this phenomenon. Although I was raised in a religious family, I was a very fearful child. (It would seem that having faith, as taught by religions, would eliminate fear.) As far back as I can remember, I was afraid of some "thing" or another that I feared may happen in the future. As I grew older and had my own family, I went from my adolescent fears such as "What if I lose my boyfriend or scholarship?" to my adult fears of "What if I lose my job or my child becomes seriously ill?"

As you can imagine, such fears can go on and on into infinity. So when I decided some years ago to begin my own spiritual journey, the first thing I wanted to work on in my consciousness was increasing my faith in God. I felt that if I really believed in God's power, I did not have to worry about the infinite numbers of "What-ifs…" I knew that I was on the right track because on my first day with my new faith-filled attitude, I experienced a miracle. I knew that God was telling me that I was on the right track.

You see, like so many people, I sped up my spiritual journey (started jogging down the path as opposed to sauntering) when I was going through a particularly difficult situation. I had retired from my federal government position because I had become ill as a result of working in a "sick building." I worked in the building for about 14 years before I began experiencing disturbing physical symptoms. Several years after the onset of these symptoms, the building was identified as a health hazard. After I left my job, I began to become fearful about my financial situation, because I had a substantially smaller amount of money coming to me every month. I thought that I had developed so much faith over the years, yet I was feeling insecure about my finances, even though my business interests were doing pretty well. However, my lack of faith in my ultimate entitlement to the abundance in God's universe prompted me to look for a part-time job.

Once the fear that I did not have enough resources took hold of my consciousness, I immediately looked for and found a job, which I really liked. Within a month of working on this new job, I began to experience the same sick building symptoms that had originally forced me into early retirement. As the universe would have it, the building where the new job was located had the same environmental problems that the building I retired from exhibited. I immediately was struck by what I thought was a coincidence. Actually, there are no coincidences. Among the lessons I learned from this situation was the realization that my search for the job demonstrated a lack of faith of God's unlimited ability to provide for me. Although it was subtle, and very deep, I knew I was experiencing that same fear that I thought I had made strides in overcoming.

Although in *my* mind I thought that I was filled with faith, some part of me must not have really believed that God was taking care of all my needs in the absolute best way. I forgot to "let go and let God."

We must realize that the path that is spiritual growth is not a straight line going forward to glory without any curves or detours.

As we are spiritual beings having a human experience, we are frequently shown that some aspect of ourselves needs more work. We can use these moments of awareness to strengthen our spirits and become better people. We should never be discouraged, but look upon these situations as opportunities to recommit ourselves to moving forward in a positive manner. If a trait that we do not like resurfaces, we should attempt to understand why and look at what is happening in our lives at that particular time. However, we must love ourselves for the many times that we functioned without exhibiting the trait and be forgiving of ourselves. Just remember that we are progressing and are becoming better people than we were previously. Life is a journey, and journeys have twists, turns, and sometimes detours. With the knowledge that God is our traveling companion, we will end our journey exactly where we are supposed to be.

Chapter 2
Bless And Honor Your Body

Several years ago, my right arm was injured. I did not know how the injury occurred. All I knew was attempts to move my arm resulted in extreme pain and part of the time I could not even use my hand. Even typing and writing resulted in discomfort. While experiencing these sensations, I began to ponder just what happens when we are forced to become acutely aware of our physical bodies, the service our bodies have given us, and the limitations we sometimes experience (such as my injury) in using these bodies.

Not being able to use my arm was extremely challenging for me. The injury prevented me from performing the myriad activities that constitute my life. The pain I experienced forced me to stop activities that involved the usage of my arm, or to at least slow down. As you can imagine, not being able to use your dominant arm or hand can really slow you down. Once I stopped and became quiet, I reflected on why I was experiencing this injury and how I could get better. Becoming quiet allowed me to hear my inner voice and brought me in touch with some latent emotions.

If you have ever had a physical injury and were unable to engage in your regular physical activities, you will remember that you found yourself with extra time on your hands. Much of the time that you previously used for doing all of your routine activities became available to you. Maybe, like me, you realized that you could use this time for inner reflection, reading, meditation, prayer or other mental/spiritual endeavors. When I took advantage of this opportunity to switch my focus from the outer to the inner, I found myself more aware of the world of "being" as opposed to the world of "doing." In the world of "being," I experienced time differently.

This newfound time can become a time of quiet and growth as well as a chance to take a spiritual leap forward. With my injured arm, I kept struggling to accept that I really did have to stop "doing" and "be" still. This was not easy for me, but once I accepted that I actually had no other choice, I really threw myself into working inwardly instead of working outwardly. Realizing and going with this became so rewarding for me.

For a brief period, I could not use my arm and hand at all. As the injured arm was my right arm, and I am right-handed, I think I learned so much more from the experience than had my left arm become nonfunctional. I began to think hard about all of the service that my right arm had given me over the years. This arm had been writing, stirring food, feeding me, changing diapers, starting my car, making jewelry, lighting candles, raising windows, and on and on and on with innumerable acts of service. It has been the "go-getter" for my body. For my entire life, it had served so much, without complaint. Now it seemed to want a rest.

I started doing work with my left arm. The left arm seemed to immediately begin saying to me: "Do not expect me to take over all that work at this late date. I have been a loyal assistant, but I will not be overused because you pushed the right arm to the point of needing a break." I noticed that the left arm started feeling tired and worn out at the slightest amount of activity.

After just one week of taking over, the left arm started feeling sore—after just one week! *It*, like the right arm, now wanted some time off.

I began to understand as never before that the body is a whole entity. Not only are the physical body parts operating as a whole, but our physical, mental, spiritual, and emotional bodies act in concert as well. Muscle tissues are connected, and overusing one part is reflected and felt in the whole. The body really has a powerful overall intelligence. In this situation, the left arm was intelligent enough to know that one of the major lessons I needed to learn in my life is to slow down and rest. So, the left arm was not about to sabotage this lesson by taking over all the physical labor, thereby enabling me to continue driving myself at my usual pace.

I began to apologize to the right arm for any abuse it had experienced from my pushing me to do more and more when it, and my entire body, desperately needed rest. I thanked this arm for the many things it has done to make my life meaningful and exciting, not to mention being key to helping my body survive. I blessed and thanked this arm and my entire body.

Perhaps you may want to take a moment now to thank and bless your entire body for its service to you. Remember, we are spiritual beings having a human experience. We need these bodies in optimal condition to have the "human" experience and to achieve our life mission and purpose. Our bodies are the vehicles that carry our spirits through the many experiences and lessons we are continually encountering while here on earth. This is a primary reason to honor our bodies with proper diet, proper exercise, much prayer, much love, and rest. We must love our bodies at whatever state or stage we are in.

Now, there are many other ways to look at my experience, and those of you who know me are aware that I have turned this experience upside down and inside out. I had thoughts about the meaning of injuring the right arm versus the left arm, the metaphysical causative factors of the injury, and the purpose of my having a period of physical inactivity. Through all of this analyzing, my foremost realization was that I needed more time to become still and introspective.

I only want to remind you to love and honor your body as the true miracle that it is. As you bless and honor your physical body with love, care, and quiet, you also bless and honor your spiritual body. When we take the time to give our physical bodies the time they need to rest and rejuvenate, our spiritual bodies have the opportunity to get more of our attention. We are in turn rewarded with more insight into our individual spirits. We learn about our inner selves, who we truly are, and that allows us to gain information about our physical selves. Then we will be able to remember that there is only one body after all—only One.

Chapter 3
Gratitude Changes Situations

A few years ago, I woke up in the middle of a winter night feeling like I was sleeping outside in a cold tent, which is something that just doesn't happen to me. By morning, still cold, I looked at my electric clock to find that there were no numbers on it. It was just sitting there giving me a blank stare, and I realized that there was no electricity running through my house. There had been an ice storm that night, so I imagined that the storm was responsible for my lack of electricity and warmth. I did not even want to get out of bed because the atmosphere was icy cold.

For about an hour, I kept thinking that the electricity would come back on at any minute. When that did not happen, I surveyed my situation to see how I could get warm. I mean, my thermostat indicated that it was only fifty-eight degrees in the house! Well, I had no firewood, and no way to get heat. I could not even get my oven to turn on. I was afraid to drive on the ice, so that meant I could not go to my mother's house (which, by the way, was warm) or anywhere else for that matter.

Thank God, I did have hot water in my hot water heater. So, I prepared myself an extremely hot bath, and put essential oils in the water in order to indulge in aromatherapy. Before I got into the hot bath, I brought incense, candles, and quartz crystals to sit on the rim of the bathtub. With all of this, I decided to just sit, be still, and meditate there.

I remember that it was very quiet because there were no sounds from the radio, television, or furnace, as they all run on electricity. My space was quiet, and it felt wonderful. I could see the steam rising from the bathtub; I was very warm and began to be transported to a place of such peace and tranquility. I even began to receive answers to questions I had asked of myself a year earlier——answers which until that morning had eluded me. The experience was absolutely stupendous.

During this period in the bathtub, while meditating, I began to feel such gratitude for the items that I had brought into the bathroom. I felt gratitude for those things that were making me feel so comfortable at the time. With the exception of the crystals, I had never thanked God for these things——the hot water, essential oils, and incense. All of them exist as parts of nature, and I realized that God always works through nature to support me——*always*.

Often we do not recognize and show gratitude for these things that we frequently think of as being small and perhaps insignificant. How often do we even express gratitude for the heat in our homes when many people live and work in the cold every day? Most of us are so blessed to have warm homes, cars, and food to eat. When I was sitting in that hot water, I was so grateful. The gratitude washed over and through me like the water I was sitting in. It was a tremendous feeling, and I realized that I should practice being more grateful for the things that I take for granted——the so-called "little things."

Gratitude involves acknowledging the gifts we have been given, realizing their true value, appreciating this value, and thanking the Creator for these gifts. Also, our gratitude is such an essential part in creating the good that God wants for all of us. For, while I was in the warm tub sincerely expressing my gratitude for the experience, guess what happened? The lights clicked back on, and the electricity was back. I was so shocked. Being thankful and not resisting my condition created the atmosphere for the problem to be corrected. If we want to experience more goodness in our lives, we need to express gratitude for the goodness that is already here, ever present.

I left the bathroom with the message that I should not wait until I am "in the dark" or uncomfortably cold before I express gratitude for all I have. God has truly allowed me to have all that I need in my life and for that, I am so grateful!!

Chapter 4
Develop More Patience

"Patience is a virtue, kindness is an act of love…" is a message that Omushaho has kept on her answering machine for as long as I can remember. The first couple of times I heard that message, besides being frustrated with the fact that I was talking to a machine and not to her, I impatiently asked myself, who ever thinks about patience anyway? What does it really mean to be patient? According to Webster's dictionary, the definition of "patience" is: (1) capable of bearing affliction calmly; (2) understanding, tolerant; (3) persevering; constant; (4) capable of bearing delay.

Actually, I had never given much thought to patience (as a virtue or otherwise) because I grew up with the idea that I had to make things happen, as soon as possible——if possible. Growing up, it seemed as though the idea of being patient somehow was akin to almost giving up. Now, being an adult, I can see how patience *is* a virtue and a necessary attribute for each of us to have in our lives.

To lack patience is to put ourselves through unnecessary turmoil and frustration. Yes, we must always do our part to see that we move successfully along our chosen paths and achieve our goals. But, we should remember that in moving along our paths, we are in partnership with God. After we put in our portion of the work, we should patiently allow God to work for us in God's time. Remembering that our lives are in Divine Order should facilitate our being patient.

Looking at the definition of "patience," I can see that it describes traits that directly correlate to our spiritual and emotional growth as well as the achievement of our goals. We cannot always have things, or responses from people, exactly when we want them. Many of us are so eager and rushed to get to some designated point that we are continually frustrated with our world. And by getting so out of "at-one-ment" with God, we rarely take time to enjoy the present moment. The following are some questions that I have asked myself in the past. Do any of them sound familiar to you?

*Why do I always end up in the slowest line in the supermarket? And, when I switch lines in order to finish faster, why do I end up being in line just as long…sometimes even longer?

*Why is the child I am with always lagging behind me? Why can't he or she walk faster, especially since we are running late?

*Why do I have to explain some action or concept to this particular person over and over again?

I found that, although the person or situation I am frustrated with may have felt some negative energy from me, whatever they felt did not seem to be as frustrating and bothersome to them as it was to me. I was causing myself turmoil! The clerk in the supermarket probably was not even aware that I felt anything, and if she were, what could she do about it anyway?

We are disturbing our own peace when we lack patience. As a result, we are disturbing our health. Maybe you have never experienced such feelings. Even if you have, perhaps you still exhibited kindness to those with whom you were losing patience.

However, there are times when being patient is much harder and the stakes are much higher. For example, many of us have experienced serious challenges in our lives that "try" our patience.

This may occur when we are searching for a new job; waiting for a promotion we deserve; or, perhaps waiting for some physical, spiritual, or emotional healing. We may have prayed and waited, and to our understanding, have seen no apparent results or answers. Do we respond by losing patience and losing faith? Do we beat up on ourselves for some action we have (or have not) taken to help the situation? Do we feel that God has not heard our plea? These are just the times when being "persevering, constant, understanding, tolerant, and capable of bearing delay" are so important.

I primarily see my impatience clearly coming forth when I just have to do that one more little thing that will speed some process along, instead of letting go and letting God. I have really had to work on this. Sometimes I become impatient with myself because I am involved in so many activities and cannot understand why I cannot take on just *one more* project! In the past, there have been times when I actually became impatient with my body's inability to work on four hours of sleep. We must not only be patient with others, but we must also learn to be patient with ourselves. Of course, we are not perfect, but we can only do the best we can and move forward in faith. We should extend the same tolerance and understanding to ourselves as we extend to others.

As we know, God always answers our prayers, but we must be patient with God also, and realize that whatever time frame and specific results we may think are needed, may not be what God has planned. God has greater plans for us than we have, or can even imagine, for ourselves. God is within each of us at all times, at every moment.

The next time you feel that things are not happening fast enough, it would be wise to think of the good that is happening at that very moment, and remind yourself that God is in charge and all is well. Your good will comes to you in God's divine time and in divine order. To this day, I remain grateful to Omushaho for the continual reminder.

Chapter 5
Create Your Desired Reality

I spent all of my childhood being a painfully shy person, but there was a part of me that desired to be outgoing. My younger sister, Denise, was constantly happily speaking to everyone she knew and even those she did not know. On the other hand, I would go out of my way not to be noticed. I had a very hard time speaking to people whether I knew them or not. I can even remember hiding from my elementary school classmates before they noticed me, if I spotted them outside of the school setting.

By the time I got to high school, I really wanted to become more personable and outgoing, so I decided that I would create a new persona. I analyzed my situation and found that, if I took off my glasses, I could enthusiastically speak to people. These people were my fellow high school classmates, so I know this may sound odd. I think that it was easier for me to speak to them because, being nearsighted, I could not see the expressions on their faces if I was not wearing eyeglasses. Seeing them as a blur made them all appear the same and made me feel comfortable enough to say something to them.

Pretty soon, I was walking up and down the halls of the school smiling and saying "Hello" to just about everyone I passed.

I felt no discomfort at all and eventually this became me. I found that more and more people reacted positively to me, and in turn, I became more at ease and more confident with my new persona. I spoke to everyone because, at a distance, I could not tell whether I knew the person or not. In later years, when my mother had occasion to see me in my work environment, she told me that she had a hard time believing that I was the same "withdrawn" Susan. By then, I was grown and my personality was much more developed. I felt much better about people in general because I was able to talk with them and get to know them.

The main point that I want to emphasize is that I wanted to relate differently to others in my environment, and I was able to change my way of being and create an environment that I wanted and that proved to serve me much better throughout my life. Changing our way of looking at situations can result in our manifesting anything we want in our lives, if we really want it. To create a condition or environment that we desire in our lives, we must act "as if"—as if it were already here. We must speak as though it is already here; feel as if it is already here, and eventually we know it *is* here.

About twenty years ago, when I first started studying metaphysics and believing that I could create my reality, I felt that I had to first really believe that whatever I wanted was already there. This is true, but at that time I kept struggling with the thought that I could not immediately see any manifestation of the change I was attempting to create. Wouldn't I see it if it was already there? I would go around and around with this concern in my head. Eventually, I accepted that although we my not see the change immediately, it is still becoming manifest in spirit. As I learned to continually believe that what I desired was happening at that very moment, and thanked God for the change, I eventually did see the manifestation. It is important to remember that when we are creating, it is actually God's presence within us that is doing the creating. Knowing that all things are possible for God, it makes it easy to know that the change is happening, as long as it is for the good.

Of course, it is great if we can believe that the change has already occurred. As we see it, speak it, and feel it, in fact the change has already occurred. To manifest a new reality, sometimes we don't immediately believe that it has already taken place, but by knowing that the condition can change, and acting as if it has, we are able to bring about the change that we desire. Do you remember when we were children and we played "pretend"? We can still do this when we act "as if."

Perhaps you may want to create more prosperity in your life. You can begin by acting as if you already have it. For example, the next time you have an opportunity to share with someone else, give of the prosperity you have in a free and loving manner. Begin to know that there is no scarcity and no limitation in God's universe. Tell yourself that the universe and your prosperity have no limits. As you freely give, freely you will receive. For it is true, you do have wealth. Remember also, that everything is circular and cyclical, and the good we extend to others is returned to us.

If you want friends, start by being the best friend you can be to someone you know and treat everyone you meet as you would like to be treated. Observe the positive reactions people have toward you, and begin seeing the good and the positive in others.

Whether we are conscious of it or not, we are creators and co-creators with God. We can consciously choose to create the more wondrous lives that we were meant to experience, or we can create the same circumstances and situations again and again. We have the power to consciously choose to create something better. Let's go for the best!

Chapter 6
Communicate Through The Spiritual Internet

Crysta@Erols.com. This was my first Internet address, and I remember countless people contacting me there. Once I got Internet service, I was continually astonished at the amount of information that was immediately available to me on almost any subject in the universe right in my own home. Even though I was happy with the ability to retrieve so much information, I was a reluctant and perplexed onlooker to the phenomenon of people being "tied" to their home computers for unbelievable amounts of time. Through the Internet, we are able to communicate with people throughout the entire world, and our lives and realities are changing daily because of this. (I cannot help but add that since the small quartz chip within the computer makes all of this possible, this is another example of the power of quartz crystals!)

In just a few years, Internet use has proliferated, and we have changed the way we handle our lives, from banking online to diagnosing our physical conditions through looking up our symptoms online. This is all very wonderful as the information can make our lives much easier.

However, we have always had access to an unlimited supply of information. Yes, this is true. Through contact with God, our unlimited source of information, and the use of our intuition, we have the perfect answers to any issue that touches our lives. This reality is so exciting to me!! I like to call this the "natural internet," or the ultimate power source. This source of information has been in effect since the beginning of time. To access the natural Internet, we do not need to call Comcast, Verizon, or Earthlink. We only need to take time each day to quiet our minds and listen to the still, small voice of God, which is always speaking to us and knows all.

How is this done? The easiest way is to set aside time for meditation every day. We can use this time to contact the Creator, God, and allow God to speak truth to us. As we become still and quiet the chatter in our minds, God's voice can be easily heard. Of course, God lives within each of us and is continually speaking to us. But it is only when we become quiet that we can hear the message. God loves us and wants us to be constantly in contact. Once connected, we can then ask questions and get the right "divine" answers. Our lives become so much more meaningful, abundant, peaceful, and joyful.

After meditating, our goal should be to maintain that connection with God at all times. We should be able to carry the aura of our Divine connection as we go through our daily activities. Staying connected can be challenging, but by doing so, we find that life issues work themselves out perfectly with very little work on our part. Our *part* is to remain in touch with God.

Many of us have regular periods of meditation and can attest to the tremendous benefit meditation has brought to our lives. I am sure you will agree that, at first, it may be difficult to quiet the mind because in most peoples' cases, the mind has been running uncontrollably rampant for so long. I used to think of my mind as a child that needed to be disciplined. Usually, this attitude of attempting to force the mind to stop thinking made it more active. If you encounter continued difficulty, try to be still and concentrate on your breathing. However, by starting out with just five minutes a day of meditation, you will find that it gets easier and easier in time, and you will look forward to those moments of peace and "knowing." Your days will go smoother leading to a life that is wonderful. Not only will answers come to you during those precious periods, but during the day, you will become aware that people and nature support you by supplying you with encouragement and answers also. That is because we, and all of nature, are connected to God and are part of this natural Internet.

I will share with you one example of how this worked in my life. Years ago, I went to Jamaica on vacation and stayed in a cabin on the beach. There were many beautiful flowering trees and much foliage surrounding the cabin. Being a city girl, however, I put lotion on my legs before I left Washington, and as soon as I arrived at the cabin in Jamaica, the insects seemed to be having my legs for dinner. I woke up the first morning with about thirty bites on my legs. I was in paradise, but I was so uncomfortable. Actually, I was miserable.

The next day while walking along a road, a Jamaican woman came up to me and spoke and proceeded to walk down the road with me. After I parted from her, she turned around and began to follow me. She started asking me about my legs and those seemingly 300 insect bites. She pulled out the largest aloe vera leaf I had ever seen and began massaging the aloe vera gel on my legs. It immediately stopped the itching. In addition, she said that I could apply the plant and the insects would stop biting me. I purchased all of the plant she had on her, cut it into small pieces, and rubbed it on my skin daily. What a blessing she had bestowed upon me!

I did not know this woman. She just appeared on the road at the start of my vacation to help me. The other part of this natural Internet of non-stop information is that the day before I left for the vacation, Nature's Sunshine Products, for which I was a consultant, sent me a *free* bottle of aloe vera gel that I packed with my other things. So, I had aloe very gel with me, but did not know all of its uses. The Jamaican woman helped to educate me when I had no computer hook-up. These are not coincidences. These are examples of God constantly connecting with us through other people and through nature to make our lives healthy and joyful.

You can now reach me at Earthlink.net, and I would love to hear from you. But don't forget to first access our natural Internet where the truth and the answers we need are on time, free, and of the highest quality. I will meet you there, too, at all times.

Chapter 7
Always Maintain A Prayerful Attitude

In terms of numerology, the year 1998 was a year of inner growth and spirituality for me. I had studied several books on numerology including *Numbers And You* by Lloyd Strayhorn, and I realized that this was a year represented by the number seven. It was a year that required going within, reflective study and self-analysis, communing with spirit, and growing spiritually. For me, the feeling I had during the year was one of intense spiritual challenge. I knew I would have to overcome these challenges in order to move successfully along my spiritual path in the succeeding years. It seemed as if every lesson I thought I had already learned resurfaced in some small way.

I meditated, prayed, and recorded my feelings and insights as a means of making the best of that year. At that time, I felt little desire to push my business and be "out in the world." During 1997, I put together numerous herbal seminars and participated in several craft and metaphysical shows to sell my jewelry creations. When 1998 arrived, I felt myself being more and more drawn within and, as a result, did only one health show during the entire year. Many times, I just hoped that I could make it through 1998.

As the year progressed, even with all the spiritual energy I did put into it, part of my internal struggle focused on my fear that I was not doing *enough* spiritual work. The year was moving on, and I had no idea as to how much spiritual work constituted "enough." By September 1998, I made a bracelet of tiny quartz crystal beads, which included little white beads that spelled out the word "PRAY."

I wore this bracelet constantly—never taking it off—to remind me to pray continuously and to develop, what I call, a "*prayerful attitude.*" With a prayerful attitude, all of the activities I performed during the day are consciously interspersed with prayer. I felt that this prayerful attitude would help keep me at an optimal spiritual level. Whenever I looked at my wrist, I was reminded to say a short prayer of thanksgiving, or a prayer for a loved one, or to bless a passerby. Eventually, I did not even have to see the bracelet to stop during the day and offer a prayer.

I came out of 1998 with increased self-knowledge and understanding. One of the things I realize is that maintaining a prayerful attitude is necessary for me *whatever* year it is. When I was a child, attending Catholic school, every hour a bell would ring, on the hour. This would signal us to stop and pray. We also prayed when we arrived at school and before we left school to return home. This may seem excessive, however, it became a matter of course for us. In many countries of the world, it is practice that people stop their activities during the day and pray.

Pausing for prayer allows me to connect with God, our Creator, and reminds me that my life and affairs are in Divine Order. I then immediately experience a higher level of peace, and an opportunity to operate from a higher level of consciousness. The activities of my life run smoother, and I am better able to discern and act out the will of God.

In maintaining a prayerful attitude, we may want to pray for relatives or friends by speaking a short affirmative statement about them. We may bless a stranger with whom we happen to come in contact. We may succinctly express gratitude for the health, prosperity, and joy that are blessings in our lives. Continually expressing gratitude for our blessings speaks to our awareness of the truth that we are truly blessed and puts us in a position to maintain and increase these blessings.

Well, some time in early 1999, the bracelet broke, some of the beads were lost, and I never repaired it. I told myself that I had achieved this prayerful attitude as a permanent part of my life and the broken bracelet was a sign that I no longer needed the bracelet as a reminder. I dropped the salvaged parts of the bracelet into a box.

Some months passed, and I realized that my prayerful attitude was somewhat slipping away. I could tell because I was becoming a little more stressed about things; a little more perplexed by some people and things; and, a little less at peace. So, I was led to make another prayer bracelet because I felt that the prayerful attitude must become a stronger and stronger part of my life, forever.

Ultimately, the prayerful attitude became a staple in my life, and I now wear the bracelet only when I feel the need to remind myself to increase the number of conscious prayerful moments in my day.

Chapter 8
Music Brings Joy And Health To Our Lives

When my sister Denise called me to tell me that she had just bought a new piano, she immediately began to recount how happy she felt playing it in the piano store. She knew she had to buy it. Since the time we were children, I had been listening to her speak of her dream of owning a baby grand piano.

Ironically, I had been in an unusually intense musical frame of mind for months prior to her purchase, so her joy was of particular interest to me. For as long as I can remember, music has been a major part of my life. As a child, I can remember my father singing hymns and spirituals on Sunday morning, usually while he was preparing a Sunday breakfast, his voice intertwining with the scent of our meal. I also remember my mother frequently singing a song entitled "Trees" to us. My parents owned these fantastic record albums, so whether I was washing dishes, doing homework, or playing with my dolls, sounds of Ahmad Jamal, Ella Fitzgerald, or Dakota Staton were my background soundtracks.

Then I remember my grandmother bringing over Brook Benton's latest 45 recording for us to hear. But, when we would visit her house, she would have us sit down and quietly listen to music from her library of classical music.

I also remember my aunt, Jane, carrying Jackie Wilson's recording of "Lonely Teardrops" in her purse. She would take the record out for Mama to play it on the stereo, and we would all jump up and dance the cha-cha around the living room.

All of us were given music lessons. Denise and I played piano; Rhonda played violin and flute; Kevin played clarinet; and Neal sang in several choirs. With seven people living in our house, there was always noise and music, noise and music. Our house was never quiet if even one of us was awake.

When I became a parent, I began to experience living with music from another vantage point. My children had their favorite artists that they listened to, and of course, I still had my favorites. They both took music lessons. My son started drumming out Go-Go beats when he was a teenager and moved on to the African rhythms he plays on his djembe to this day. Sometimes these rhythms served as my wake-up call in the morning. This was an infectious, new form of music for me.

Most of us who grew up in black families have, perhaps, experienced similar situations. Your experience may not have been as intense as mine because, let's face it, how many families have seven people living in a house where five of them are noisy children? But the harmony and cacophony of sound was my life and the only life I knew.

Throughout my life, music has kept me going when I thought I did not have the energy to continue. Music has brought exuberance to an already fantastic day or event. As a child, if I was punished for some wrongdoing, music was my comfort. If I were sad, I had music to sing or play which uplifted me, and if I was happy, I had music to dance to. I learned early in life that music could alter my mood and my environment.

Life *is* sound.   Anyone who has undergone a medical ultrasound procedure understands this profound truth without any explanation from me.   Even when *we* are quiet, the sounds of the universe are constantly vibrating around us.   With inner quiet, we can tune into these sounds.   So when we are still and quiet, there are an infinite number of earth sounds affecting us——the wind blowing, the leaves rustling, the birds chirping, and the roar of the ocean.   These sounds are gifts to us from our universe.

Music can alter our moods.   It can bring joy; put us into a meditative, prayerful state; and, bring back forgotten memories and feelings.   The vibration of sound can change the structure and responses of our bodies.   This fact is the basis for music therapy.

So, if I am sluggish or tired, the fast-paced, driving, thumping sounds of African drumming awakens that life force in me and gets me going.   Try listening to these sounds when you are engaged in physical exercise, as opposed to something more sedate, and notice how much longer you can exercise.   On the other hand, if I am stressed or anxious, I choose to hear light jazz or classical melodies.   These sounds tend to calm and soothe my nerves and put me in a quieter state of being.

A drum rhythm can be felt in the soul and has a real connection to the earth and our earthiness.   I immediately feel this sound in my base chakra, in the depth of my being, and the energy seems to move up from the earth through my feet and lungs.   On the other hand, a high-pitched soprano sax or violin sound is felt in my crown or intuitive energy centers.   I experience these sounds as opening up these centers that are more connected with spirituality and knowing.   All of the chakras, the energy centers of the body, are affected by sound and tones.   Each of the seven major chakras relates to the seven main notes of the musical scale.   Therefore, even singing a particular tone or note can have a healing, mood-altering effect on the physical, emotional, and spiritual aspects of the body.

Music and sound are clearly blessings to us that we should consciously avail ourselves of these blessings whenever we have the opportunity. Even if we have no instruments or recorded music to play, we can sing and create our own particular sound. Our bodies themselves are vibrating instruments.

Now, I live in a quiet home; there is only the sound and the music that I create. I now understand the beauty of silence, but it took years and years to achieve that appreciation. Silence brings with it a peace and an ability to hear my inner voice as I could have never heard it years ago. Nevertheless, I forever know the beauty of sound. The conscious use of both silence and sound provide the balance and health that is needed for our bodies, minds, and spirits.

Of course, I love, and frequently miss, the music and spirit of the family members with whom I once lived. Looking back, I am feeling those times as a series of profound symphonies— each member of the family representing a different sound or instrument. But whether you or I live with a symphony or a solo, our lives are always enhanced by music. What a blessing!

Chapter 9
Infuse Your Life With Childlike Energy

"Suffer little children to come unto me, and forbid them not: for of such is the kingdom of God" [Luke 18:16]. Many of us have heard this Bible quotation from childhood into adulthood. As a child, I remember hearing this from my grandfather, who was the pastor of a church. At the time, I thought being a child afforded me a better chance to get into heaven and to be with God. In my mind at the time, this seemed perfectly logical because children had not lived long enough to accumulate the number of "sins" that adults had been here long enough to accumulate.

As I have matured into adulthood, I see this Bible passage in a different light. I first became conscious of my new viewpoint after Sekou, my first grandchild, was born. I took the time to observe his behavior as a baby and as a toddler. Through him, I have been blessed with the opportunity to learn so much. By the time he was eighteen months old, I began to ask myself these questions: "What does it mean to be a child?" "Why does the Bible passage imply that we must be as children to be with God?" "What are the characteristics that I see in children that are frequently lost as we enter adulthood?" Upon reflection, I have noticed that the following traits are frequently found in children. I believe that it is not the lack of an accumulation of misdeeds that affords the young easy access to heaven, but rather that their way of being is more closely related to God's spirit.

1. **A Sense of Wonder and Awe**. We should have an exceptional appreciation for God's universe and the magic that lies within it. My grandson does. As we walk through the park, he picks up rocks, sticks, and even takes them home. (Remember that the Kingdom of God is "at hand.") He looks to the sky and tells me about the trees, sometimes he comments on each tree as we pass. It appears that he is seeing the awesomeness of God in everything he encounters.

2. **Being Forgiving**. We must release any negative feelings about perceived wrongs that have been done to us. This is not so much for the benefit of the other person or circumstance, as it is for us. Forgiveness enhances the presence of God within us and affords us peace. Sekou sometimes gets upset if he is not allowed to do what he wants. Once, I told him not to open the door and, in response, he fell out on the floor. After I talked with him, he hugged me and put his head on my lap-—all within about two minutes from the tantrum to the embrace. How many days or years do adults hold grudges against one another?

3. **Being Energetic**. We must develop and inject an energetic attitude in all that we do and try to feel excited and proud of our existence and of what we accomplish. I am sure all of you have seen young children as they go about their activities. They are the epitome of unbridled energy. The universe and all life is quite simply *energy*. To be successful and prosperous in or lives, we should energetically infuse all of our activities with an excitement for life—whether our activities are recreational or occupational in nature. We, thereby, stay in flow with the universe. Sekou runs

almost everywhere he goes; sometimes he stops and jumps up in the air several times—just because he can do this! And when he accomplishes a new activity, he applauds himself saying, "yeah," along with us. Believe me, if we don't applaud him, he will applaud himself, *all by himself*. He is fascinated with the universe—and *he* is fascinating.

4. **Being Open-minded**. We should be willing to accept people, places, and things without prejudice and judgment. The act of judgment causes us discomfort and unhappiness. This includes being open, receptive, and willing to learn new things and to change ourselves, if necessary. Sekou learns from all people and all situations. He is able to accept each experience as a learning one, take what he can from the experience, and move to a higher level.

5. **Having a Lack of Fear**. Of course, it is usually easier to be fearless when we are young because we have not had countless years of admonitions and warnings from parents, community, and the media about what will happen to us "if…" But fear paralyzes us and prevents us from moving forward along our paths, as we should. God's love for us should banish our fear. Sekou will go with me wherever I take him without concern for how fast we go or what will happen when we reach our destination. As a matter of fact, he pretty much enjoys the trip to wherever! Are we fearlessly enjoying our lives—our trip?

6. **Be Trusting**. Many of us do not trust our universe. As a general attitude, we frequently think someone, or something, is trying to do us harm, or take from us. Of course, if we have experienced negative situations from a particular person, we need not put ourselves in the same situation again. But, any lack of trust we have is ultimately a lack of trust in God's ability to care for us. God is always within us, around us, protecting and

prospering us. By trusting the power of God within, we learn to trust the universe around us. Believe me, having constant mistrust in our consciousness *creates* situations that warrant mistrust. We frequently then find our perception of the universe materializes. Sekou knows that we will take care of him, and we do. He does not doubt this.

7. **Love**. Although I am mentioning this trait last, love for God's universe, which constitutes the people, places, and things around us, moves us a long way toward living in God's light and entering the "Kingdom of Heaven." (Remember again, the Kingdom of God is at hand.) Loving actually constitutes being one with God. We can do this by seeing the God presence in every part of creation, and specifically seeing the Christ in each person. Sekou does this effortlessly. Actually, if we can accomplish this, we will have a sense of wonder, trust, forgiveness, energy, and lack of fear and prejudice.

I am so grateful that Sekou, and my five other grandchildren, are in my life. I wrote this piece when he was my only grandchild and every moment with him was one of adventure, wonder, learning, and unconditional love. Do yourself a favor and take the opportunity to share time with a child whether the child is a relative or an acquaintance. You will discover, or perhaps rediscover, a piece of God's spirit.

Chapter 10
Be Prepared For Constant Change

Many times I find myself reflecting on the fact that life seems so illusionary. During certain periods of my life I am moving along, or seemingly so, and I come to a point where I ask myself, "How did I get here?" It seems like yesterday I was over there, and now I am here? "Yesterday" could have been months or years ago, but the illusion is that it was just a short moment ago.

I usually do not ask these questions when the shift has put me in some wonderful place. I just seem to take for granted that these good things are supposed to happen. But, when I find that I am in some undesirable space—all of the questions begin. How did this happen? When did this happen? Why did this happen to me? My feeling is that the questioning starts because life is forever changing and shifting. The change happens moment by moment, and is usually subtle.

Do you remember playing with a kaleidoscope when you were a child? I loved kaleidoscopes as a young person and still love them. There are so many colors at the bottom of the tube, and I could never figure out how they got there. However, as I turned the bottom, the colors began to shift. The shift revealed a new pattern—same colors but the pattern and texture of what I saw had changed. My turning of the kaleidoscope and the subsequent change may have been ever so slight, but I saw a beautiful new pattern. To think of it still lights up my mind. Recently, I was given a kaleidoscope as a gift, and I still do not understand how the myriad of beautiful shapes and patterns manifest.

I liken the experience of "How did I get here?" to the kaleidoscope. Every moment of our lives contains changes. We may wake up tomorrow and find that although it is another day, we have the same job, the same house, the same children, or whatever. This is an illusion. It is not so—not in reality. Just as the Earth continues to move around the sun, things are continually moving in our lives. Just as the weather and the seasons change, the texture of our lives changes also.

We do not wake up on June 21 and immediately know that what we call summer has finally arrived because the foliage and temperature is probably the same as it was on June 20. So it is with our lives. Because of the subtlety of the change, the illusion for us is that for days, weeks, or even years may be that things are pretty much the same until some notable event occurs. When this seemingly new thing happens, we step outside of ourselves and observe our situation, then we will find that the change has been happening and did *not just* happen. And, the change has been our creation.

The real purpose of this discussion is linked to my earlier statement that these realizations usually occur when something we perceived as undesirable happens. When we are a little beside ourselves off-center, the questioning begins—*hopefully*.

I remember some years ago, when I was married, my husband and I went on a vacation to the beach. He was an excellent swimmer, and I am a swimmer, but one that never feels really comfortable swimming in the ocean. He asked me to stand at a particular point in the ocean and told me that he would swim further out from where I stood. I was to be his marker of how far he could swim. You may find it humorous, but I agreed to his request.

Well, he started swimming out, and large waves would come up and consistently knock me down. I would stand back up and still see him swimming farther out into the ocean. After wave number six or seven knocked me down, I was terrified to find that there was not sand beneath my feet, only some very deep water. I remember my toes reaching and reaching for the bottom of the ocean. Once I realized that there *was* no bottom for me at the moment, I knew that I was going to have to swim. So, I fearfully and frantically turned and swam to shore.

This is the way life is. We may feel that we are stable in our usual space, standing vigilant, on solid ground as the waves of everyday life come and go. But this is an illusion. As the ocean seemingly remains in place, it is actually shifting. A footnote, which I did not realize while in that ocean many years ago, is that most likely my fear of being in deep water created my experience of being shifted into the deep water. If we are not completely conscious of our surroundings and ourselves in the moment, we may find ourselves somewhere we do not want to be. We are then in the deep end of life and wondering how we got there.

The shift is happening even as I am writing. The fact that I may be unaware does not mean that it is not happening. However, I feel there are things that we can do to minimize the trauma of discovering that we have arrived in a challenging place.

We must recognize that things are constantly changing even though we may not see or recognize the changes. This is the way life is, and life is an illusion. Illusion, to me, means that things are not as we may think they are. We should be flexible and pliable. We must be able to bend with the change so that we do not break like a tree in the winds of a hurricane. So, we recognize the change and move with what is happening.

We also must be observant of our particular situations as we move through life. We should be watchful of what is going on around us. Periodically, we can ask ourselves how we are contributing to particular situations that show up in our lives and how we feel about these situations. Pay attention. We can use the intuitive powers that we all possess. Knowing does not always have to involve only our physical senses.

Most importantly, we must stay connected with the Creator at all times. Actually, our lives are like plays. These changes can be considered set and character changes. This is part of the illusion of life that we define as reality. The only reality is that there exists a Creator, God, the Great Spirit, and therein likes the stability, unchangeability, and good that most of us so desire. Our connection with this unchangeable source of energy is what enables us to see these "how did I get here" situations as just another stop on our path as we move forward into more light. Remember, at the end of the play, the lights come on, the characters take a bow, and everyone moves off stage.

I am sure that each of us is in some particular drama in our very own life play at this very moment. Try to step up from the drama and observe. What do you see? Is it reality? Can you change it? We know that eventually, of course, all will change. But with the help of God, we can co-create the change that we desire.

As with the kaleidoscope, we can initiate a change and the change can be beautiful! But, in the example I gave of the ocean, the changing forces of nature that are constantly at work knocked me around. I kept getting up and even survived the depths of the ocean. It was not as pretty as the kaleidoscope, but I survived. A good question in this regard is do we want to be proactive or reactive in life? The bottom line is that the shift may be subtle, slow, sudden, or swift—but nothing remains unchanged but God, the Creator of all. Anchor your vessel to the Creator of this wondrous universe and enjoy the trip.

Chapter 11
Joy Is Our Birthright

During the day-to-day, week-to-week, month-to-month events of our lives, it is sometimes difficult to maintain the joy of living that is our natural right. Some of us have the idea that joy is only supposed to occur sporadically—every now and then. Many feel that continuous joy and happiness are unattainable. In fact, I would venture to say that, at any moment in time, all of us might experience events that evoke feelings of frustration, worry, anger, anxiety, depression, or some other negative feeling.

These negative feelings, however, are not meant to remain a permanent condition, and once we experience these feelings we should be able to return to a joyful state. Sometimes we experience the feelings for only a second, sometimes a minute, a day, or a week; but we should be able to come back to an inner feeling of joy and peace.

As we do our spiritual work, and grow in spirit, we can have unsettling experiences and *still* be in a state of joy while experiencing them. This occurs because we realize that, on a whole, our lives are in Divine Order, and basically, all is well. We do our work, let go and let God, realizing that God maintains order in the universe. We are part of the universe, and we, too, are in order. We must continually recognize our connection with the Divine.

Besides whatever I may do spiritually to maintain joy, I have found that there are particular parts of our universe that inspire me and help to support a consciousness and feeling of joy. I see that inspiration abounds around me and through me. The following are some of my favorite sources of inspiration that joy is an entitlement and that return me to a joyful state.

The Sun. Every day the sun rises. This is, to me, a supreme example of Divine Order. The sun's radiance and warmth energize me and provide me with instant feelings of joy. Watching the sun appear on the horizon is truly an inspirational event. The dark sky begins to show hues of red, orange, and yellow. I am reminded that the sun unceasingly gives life to all things. The colors at sunrise and sunset: red, orange, and yellow all relate to the first three energy centers (chakras) of our bodies. This solar display of color and light brings energy and joy into our beings.

If you cannot be outside to witness this event, open your blinds as early as possible and allow the sunlight to shine upon you. Let its rays become absorbed into your body. I guarantee that you will immediately feel more joyful. During the warmer weather, walk or sit outside in the sun and you will begin to notice a difference in your outlook on life.

The Moon. Whenever the moon is visible, spend a few minutes basking in its glow. The moon speaks to the emotional side of our being and communicates with us on a very deep level. To me, it speaks through my inner thoughts and desires, and provides healing, as well. If you cannot go outdoors, try to let the moonlight stream through a window in your house. As with the sun, stand or sit in its glow. Watch the moon, and it will still you, bring you serenity, and speak to you. Although it may not communicate audibly, its voice seems to present itself as an inner awareness about personal issues or feelings that are on your mind or heart.

Plants, Flowers, and Trees. Plants and flowers have inspired most of us. In my opinion, the plant kingdom *is* joy in concrete, physical form. Many of us have plants in our homes and offices. They physically provide oxygen to our space and their green color is the color of health, balance, and love. Study them. Aren't they magnificent in their being! Allow their energy to blend into your energy and feel their presence as their leaves reach out to you.

Flowers, or cut blossoms, bring joy into our lives as well. I remember buying fresh flowers every week when I worked downtown. Many times the man who sold the flowers would just give me the flowers as a gift. I suppose he could see the joy in my face as I took in their beauty. We know that the color, scent, and essential oils of the flowers and plants assist in uplifting and healing our bodies, minds, and spirits.

We also experience joy from trees. We may not be as much aware of the effect and contribution of trees as we are with plants and flowers. However, we only have to remember how much peace and joy we feel when we enter a park or the woods. We feel renewed and at one with nature. A dear friend once told me that the branches of trees seem to represent the nerves and nerve endings of our physical bodies. Being among trees definitely has a positive, soothing effect on my nerves and makes me happy and serene.

Trees represent the cycle of life as they continually change and grow with the passing seasons. They inspire us to withstand life's challenges, as they stand tall through heat, cold, snow, ice, and wind. The next time you come close to a tree, try touching it, and imagine its strength flowing to you.

Music. We have all experienced the joy of music, and have our particular musical pieces that are uplifting and/or remind us of happy events and experiences. The subconscious mind, and I believe the cells of our body also, associates these pieces with the happy experiences. Therefore, if we feel less than joyful, we can play these songs to bring ourselves into a happier state.

For thousands of years, we have been aware of the ability that music has to heal. Our ears are not only our main organs for hearing, but they are also able to influence eye movement, rhythms of the physical body, and stress levels in the body. There is an entire study of sound and music therapy and the healing power of sound. However, we should just play the music that makes us feel good, especially pieces that we can relate to joyful times and experiences. This is an easy way to bring more joy into your life.

Inspirational Reading. Reading inspirational material is also a great help to us in maintaining our joy. The market is flooded with spiritual books and magazines, many of which have short positive daily messages. Also, most religions have their holy books, which have inspired followers for ages. As we read and meditate on these positive messages, we experience peace within, and this peace is a joyous blessing in and of itself.

Conversely, we may want to stay away from writings and television programs that promote negative images for us and interfere with our joyful state. Sometimes the media works on our emotions and spirits in a way in which we are not conscious. If we begin feeling fear, anxiety, or anything unsettling that is not explainable, we should make sure that we are not allowing negative images from television, newspapers, or whatever, to disturb our peace and joy. Sometimes we should just turn off our televisions.

There are, of course, many other aspects to life that provide us with joy and happiness. Certainly, we should surround ourselves with other positive people who encourage us and foster our feeling joy and worthiness within us. I will not go into detail about the role of other people because too frequently we fall into believing that other people should be responsible for providing our joy, or that others can take that joy away from us.

Actually, we are responsible for our joy and another person can never take true joy away from us unless we allow this. This is sometimes a difficult concept to accept and harder to live out.

I find that joy is found when we live in harmony with nature and our environment. This is our responsibility and our entitlement. As we do this, and experience joy, we undoubtedly attract more joyful people into our lives.

There are many other facts of the universe that produce and enhance joy that I have not mentioned. We should remain conscious of as many of them as possible and partake of those things that provide us with joy and peace, whatever those things may be. In so doing, we will find life more fulfilling and we become joy and a joy to others.

Chapter 12
Strengthen Your Connection With The Divine

Whenever some natural disaster occurs, the media, through newspapers, television, and magazines shows us countless images of the victims and casualties of these disasters. I remember the scenes of devastation and destruction left by Hurricane Katrina in New Orleans in 2005.

Many people wondered how such destruction and death could take place and why more could not have been done to prevent some of the flooding and tremendous impact on New Orleans and its people. It was also questioned why more could not have been done after the hurricane to alleviate the suffering of the people there, who was at fault for the lack of aid to the victims, and why did the government fail in its role? The pictures of people without homes, food, or loved ones were simply heartbreaking. To this day, there are still homes and areas that have not been brought back.

Other hurricanes have come and gone, as have earthquakes and tornadoes; and, more people have lost their lives and property.

Crime is increasing in our communities. Young people are not being educated well so we worry about our future generations. And let us not forget the current war in Iraq. All of this is extremely disturbing, and many of us tried to help those impacted and find answers to our nagging questions in the best way that we could. Sometimes we wondered what we could do if we had been faced with such challenges.

Could these natural occurrences be symptoms of the "last days" or are they a result of nature's response to global warming and/or environmental pollution, or just *what*? Whatever the answer, we must believe that God is still in charge, and we must remain connected to God as the One Power. At this time, people are seemingly becoming more confused, frustrated, and unhappy as they attempt to make sense of things and to hold on to the aspects of life that make them feel secure. It is now that we, as spiritual light beings, must successfully maneuver through these changes and help others along the way. It is time for us to allow our light to radiate even more. We can do this if we strengthen our Divine connection with God and allow ourselves to be vessels through which God's light will shine.

In my opinion, all events and their effects are moving faster in time, and this tends to have a dizzying effect on our emotions and spirits. This seems especially true as we witness more disastrous situations and suffering. I have spoken to many people who are experiencing more feelings of sadness, isolation, bewilderment, and confusion. I, myself, have had to put more effort into remaining centered and focused. This is precisely the time when all of us should slow down and strengthen our Divine connection. Whatever method we use to reach out, and within, to the Creator, is obviously so important for us to do so right now.

As we see the images of suffering people and desire to help them, we are reminded that we are compassionate beings. This compassion is a part of the light that we shine on those around us. Tremendous changes are taking place, however, we will survive, move forward, and assist others in doing the same. This is what we have been spiritually preparing ourselves for during the time we have been here. This may not be an easy task, but by continuously maintaining our Divine connection, we can channel and share even more of God's light.

I frequently talk about prayer, being still, meditation, and other ways to connect with God. I am inspired to do this because I have experienced spiritual, emotional, and physical challenges in my life whereby these practices have saved me and made me a stronger person. I am very serious about giving you this message and have been led to do so because I feel the intense spiritual energy and tension that is building up in the universe at this time. I can see, and you probably can too, many serious manifestations of this buildup taking place in the world today.

All of us need to stay in constant contact with God so that we may know how to act and what to do during this crucial time. We may, like many of the people that we have seen and read about, have to make quick decisions about how to proceed with our lives. The amount of time we used in times past to think about and analyze our situations may not be available to us in the future. Maintaining a continuous, prayerful attitude will enable us to intuitively see and choose the course that God wants us to follow. Our intuition and that still small voice within become so important, and we must be prepared to listen and act on them.

I realize that I, and many others, may not have concrete answers for what is going on in the world, or even in our community at this time. I so wish that I could —right here, right now—tell you the secret that would make **all** of our lives perfect or at least return them to some previously experienced state of calm or perceived normalcy. The only consolation I can offer you, as truth, is that *God is still in charge*. To survive and thrive during this time, we must know this with every fiber of our being. I know that through all of the turmoil going on now, we can remain strong if we strengthen our Divine connection. We can spiritually transcend the apparent disorder by affirming that Divine Order is blessing all situations. Knowing this, we can then let go of fear and worry and embrace love and peace. Through all of this we will be challenged, but by holding on to our connection with God and God's eternal love, we will win!

Chapter 13
Are We Helping?

When my oldest grandchildren, Sekou and Semira, were both under three years old, Sekou, my grandson, said something to me that stuck in my mind for a very long time. At the time, I was putting them both into my car. Because they were both toddlers, I developed a specific process for securing them in their car seats. I would tell Sekou to sit in the front seat of the car so that he would not run into the street, while I fastened Semira into her car seat. Once Semira was secure, I would put Sekou in the back seat and fasten him in.

On this particular day, while I was securing Semira in her seat, Sekou leaped over the front seat, jumped into his car seat and then pulled the guardrail of his seat down in front of him. He said, "I can do this all by myself," with a self-satisfied look on his face. I noticed that he had gotten into his seat so quickly that I had not even finished taking care of Semira.

Astonished, I praised him for his accomplishment and told him that he was such a big boy. Semira and I proceeded to applaud him. As she and I clapped and cheered, he said in a quietly serious voice, "I try to help, and help, and help." At this point he appeared so self-satisfied and as mature as an adult. I told him that what he had done was wonderful.

Days later, the words "I try to help, and help, and help" kept ringing in my head and I could not seem to get them out of my mind. I wondered how many of us, as adults, try to help and help and help? Do we help ourselves? Do we help others? Do we help the Earth? At two years old, Sekou was not only trying to help – he *was helping*.

As his statement kept running through my mind day after day, I thought about the meaning of "helping." What is helping? Some of us help in large, obvious ways, such as caring for an elderly relative or friend, providing transportation for those without it, raising or being a mentor to children in order to instill positive values and principles within them. These actions require us to have strength and require us to give of our time. The results are obvious, and rewarding, to us and to those people who receive our help.

It occurred to me that there are other ways to help which take very little time. The following came to my mind as examples of how we can do this.

Offer Words of Encouragement. The stress of everyday living is often accompanied by frustration, fear, and anxiety. Many of our friends and acquaintances are sometimes overwhelmed with the events of their lives. We can help them by speaking words of encouragement to them and affirming for them that their lives are in Divine Order. It can also be helpful to suggest ways that we overcame similar challenges. It is especially helpful to encourage children, as they are inheriting many of the stresses that we, their elders, have created.

Do Not Criticize. We all, at times, judge people and their actions. This really seems as though we are expecting others to live according to the ideas, principles, and standards we hold dear. This is unfair to them and to us. Of course, there are times when some criticism may be warranted. This may occur in employer/employee, parent/child, and teacher/student situations. Even then we should remind ourselves to criticize with a loving heart, and be mindful not to trample on the egos and self-esteem of others.

Listen and Be Supportive. There were times that someone has come to me with an issue important to him or her, and I have not completely listened to what that person was saying. My mind may have started wandering in five different directions and I have thus not given them my full attention. It is a gift, however, to listen to them and give them our attention and our time. We do not have to *solve* their problems, just *listen*. Sometimes as we listen and pay attention, they are listening to themselves and solving their problems even as they speak.

Bless All of Those Around You. This is extremely helpful and pretty easy to do. You can bless people silently or aloud. There are so many people walking around who are ill, depressed, unhappy, or stressed out. Send them your blessings and surround them with light and love.

Volunteer Your Time. There are many organizations that deliver worthwhile services to those in need in our community. Some of them house and feed the homeless, minister to the sick, counsel battered women, tutor children, for example. Volunteering a couple of hours of your time can mean a world of difference to another human being. It can be extremely rewarding, and in addition, I found that volunteering taught me much about myself of which I was unaware. Actually, most of us have friends and relatives that need assistance and we can volunteer to assist them with what they need.

Pray for the Earth and for One Another. We all pray for our loved ones. This helps us maintain a spiritual connection to them and bring about positive outcomes in their lives and in our own lives. However, many of us forget to pray for those with whom we are not so close, or people whom we may not like. Praying for others is the best way to enhance and heal our relationships with them.

The Earth also needs our prayers. It is alive and it feeds us, heals us, and is our home. It is suffering from our misuse and neglect of its resources, and we are beginning to see and feel the effects of this. Let's begin to pray for Earth's healing and give thanks for the many gifts the Earth continually provides. Let's also do our part to protect the Earth. We will all benefit from this action.

Well, a few weeks after Sekou proclaimed his desire to help and help, I saw little Semira with a paper towel wiping up crumbs she had dropped on the floor. When my mother and I told her to put the towel in the trash, she walked into the kitchen and did just that. We were so surprised because she was only fifteen months old at the time and really did not talk. I realized that she wanted to help also—so naturally. Many of the children on Earth now want to help; they are just waiting for our suggestion, approval, guidance, and most importantly, our example. We can give them all this, be an example for them, and expectantly watch as our world changes.

Chapter 14
Find Your Tree

One summer day, while I was looking out of my window, I was taken aback by how vibrantly green everything appeared. I remembered approaching this house before I purchased it and recalled the first thing I saw was the huge, vibrant evergreen tree in my front yard. It seemed to be the most gorgeous, welcoming tree I had ever seen. Through the years, the tree has stood outside my bedroom window. It stands tall—probably becoming taller and taller each year. However, I have no way to discern its growth. I just know that it "stands," and that I can no longer see its apex through my window.

As my children grew into adulthood, this tree remained standing. I passed the tree on my way to the car innumerable times either while just running errands or for special occasions like my children's weddings. My children passed it on the way to school, and my grandchildren love gathering its cones when they fall to the ground. Gratefully, it continues to stand tall.

For me, it symbolizes life and strength. It invites the robins, doves, blue jays, crows, and cardinals to perch on its limbs and to rest or socialize. In the morning, the squirrels chase one another from limb to limb. The tree invited me to hang a bird feeder from one of its branches. Because of its invitation, I get to feed the birds and get to know them. I am awakened each morning with bird songs, which continually bring me joy. Upon awakening I see a tiny spark of light shining through the tree, which rises to higher and higher branches. Finally, this light, which is the sun, is blazing overhead, but I realize that the tree has allowed this light to gently awaken me to consciousness by lovingly filtering its rays.

This tree reaches forever out into the community, forever stretching. Over time, the reach has become higher and higher into the sky while deeper and deeper into the earth. It is always green, not just in the spring and summer months, and this particular quality inspires the ideals of health and strength.

A couple of years ago, the hurricane raged through my area, and not one limb fell off this tree. Icicles decorate its limbs in the winter months, making the tree look like a crystal work of art. I sometimes wonder if it will freeze to death, but once the ice melts, the tree continues to thrive. Winds come, and the tree sways and bends with the wind, but it never breaks. It may shed a few needles periodically, but that seems to be its method of grooming, purging and maintaining its health and beauty.

The time the tree and I have been together represents only a small portion of its life, but during this time, I have come to identify with the tree. It speaks to me about being strong and flexible. There is so much to learn from all of nature of which this tree is a part. I, too, want to reach higher and higher levels of emotional and spiritual growth while at the same time, reaching deeper and deeper toward groundedness and centeredness. I desire to branch out while maintaining the appropriate balance just like the tree.

I want to reach out to those around me and offer support just as the tree supports the birds, squirrels, me, and other life forms around it. Like the tree, I want to be able to weather all the storms of life, the cold, icy experiences, and not just survive but to grow stronger. Just as the tree loses its needles, I attempt to shed all that is not positive and not of love.

I love my tree. God lives in this tree and in all of nature. There are millions and millions of trees that support and reflect life in our universe. We, and the trees, are all part of the same universal life. On this day, I honor that tree and the tree inside of me. Look around you and find your tree, or whatever part of nature inspires you to be the best you want to be.

Chapter 15
Stay In The Present Moment

One morning I awoke believing that it was Sunday when it was actually Monday. After realizing it was in fact Monday, I began thinking of my past week and all the enjoyable moments I had experienced. My mind then jumped to thinking about all the things I needed to accomplish in the coming week before leaving for New York on the upcoming Friday. I could subtly—very subtly—feel my emotions shifting from joy and contentment to expectation, responsibility, frustration, and tension. As was usual for me, the culminating thought was "How will I accomplish all of these things in such a short span of time?" Believe me, I was already tired, and I had not even gotten out of my bed! And, mind you, all of this occurred in a matter of about one minute— only sixty seconds.

Sometimes, this going back and forth in time, and the ensuing shift in emotions, occurs in less than sixty seconds. Sometimes it may take a longer amount of time. But, when I start taking longer amounts of time to go through all the things I have to do in the future, I become really frustrated with myself. I then begin to feel that I am using up precious minutes just thinking about what I need to do, and this certainly does not seem to be accomplishing anything. This jumping from thinking about the past to thinking about the future can create mental fatigue and anxiety.

About ten years ago, one of the spiritual concepts I discovered involved living in the present moment. As I studied this concept, I began to recognize how living in the present moment offered the promise of peace and tranquility. The idea of simply dealing with "now" was indeed a revolutionary idea for me. Actually, it took a while for me to even *understand* the concept. As I explored being in the now, or present, I encountered what seemed to be a couple of mental challenges.

I had been living with the idea that we should review our past in order to identify our past mistakes and accomplishes. This would also enable us to forgive others, if necessary, and to forgive ourselves. In addition, I thought analyzing the past enabled us to determine if we had been following our chosen life paths, moving in the right direction, and ultimately benefiting from our life "lessons." Most of our parents had warned us not to repeat the same mistakes. Even the psychological therapies involve looking at *something* in the past.

Then there is the future. Now I will confess to you that this was my biggest hurdle to staying in the present moment. I am not a linger-in-the-past-type person, but staying out of the future is a challenge for me. In my mind, that is where all possibilities exist. As a child, my mind probably spent more time in the future than in the present and past combined.

As children, we were told that our whole lives were in front of us. We were told to educate ourselves and acquire knowledge and skills in the present so that we could reap the benefits from our work in the future. Then we would grow up and take care of ourselves. How many of us spent many childhood hours daydreaming of a future where we could leave our parents, be on our own, and do just what we wanted to do? I know that I did.

But then, I also worried about the future, since neither I, nor anyone else, really knew what the future actually held. I worried about what I would do if this or that happened in the future, or how could I prevent, or prepare for, the unknown occurrences of the future. Growing up, much of my time was spent in this area, and I can now say that probably ninety-five percent of these worries never occurred. But the worrying itself brought on its own level of discomfort, even if the feared events never occurred.

How, then, do we stay in the present moment, in a peaceful state; forgive our past; enjoy past remembrances; dream and create a future; and set future goals? To me, the answer is that we must do these things while being and remaining in the present moment. We must remain grounded and present right where we are in every moment of time. We understand that the past is gone and the future has not occurred. We know that we are *right here, right now,* while observing these past and future thoughts. We do not let our minds take control and go running off with thoughts that are not productive and not under our control.

Someone said that the present is a gift, that's why a gift is called the "present." I know that the present is really all that we have. The past may be remembered and interpreted in various ways. The future has not even happened. The present is happening now at this very moment and it is beautiful!

When I first attempted to live in the present moment, I observed my thoughts running away with me and, in turn, running *me.* I would ask myself, "How do I feel right now?" This would immediately bring me into the present, and usually the answer I heard was "I feel fine." I quickly realized that, for me, much of my racing thoughts and subsequent anxiety or nervousness stemmed from thinking of the past or future.

For me, at the moment I ask myself how do I feel right now, I experience a momentary suspension of thinking. My mind becomes quiet, and I begin to feel better. My mental, thinking body gives way to my emotional, feeling body. Once I stop thinking for a second, and begin noticing how I feel, I know all is well and my tranquility is restored. Living in the present is optimal. Peace is usually found in the present.

Unless you are undergoing professional mental therapy, the past does not need much attention. We can forgive ourselves, and others, for past mistakes and learn from them without going over the details over and over again. We need not spend much time there because it has "passed." Life is about change, growth, and flowing—so it is best not to get stuck in the past. Forgive and move on.

The future needs some thought. But, I suggest that this be an organized way of thinking. Set aside a special time to make plans for future activities, how to achieve future goals, and how to create future dreams. Perhaps this can be a time before or after prayer or meditation. This would be a wonderful time to consciously speak forth the intentions you have for your life when you and your environment are centered, clear, and at peace. Again, do not get stuck in future thinking—see it and connect with it, while remaining in the present. Future dreams are created, and goals are accomplished, in the present, moment by moment.

When I follow this way of being, I notice how productive I am, and how good I feel. I am a more peaceful person, and I feel more at peace. All of my senses are open and functional. I derive more benefit from the sights, sounds, and feelings of the universe around me. Of course, there are times my mind still wanders, but if I begin feeling anxious or off-centered, I gently attempt to bring myself back into the present moment.

In studying Unity principles, I was taught that "I am" refers to God and should always be followed by a positive statement. We frequently use "I am" as an opening statement of the present moment. God is present in the eternal *now*.

We are all moving into more challenging times and it is helpful to remember not to let our minds run away with us. The culture in which we live places a high value and reward on the intellect which represents the thinking or mental body. In my opinion, the emotional and spiritual bodies have more influence on who we are. The mind is a powerful tool for us to use, but it is not *us*. If we stay in the present moment, make positive life-affirming statements, and remain aware that the present is indeed a blessed gift, we can move closer to that eternal peace that we so desire and so deserve.

Chapter 16
Begin To Enjoy Your Employment

It has been several years since I ended my twenty-seven-year career with the federal government. Every now and then I reflect back to that time and it sometimes seems like a whole other lifetime. Although it seems far away, the memories are very clear. Perhaps this is because so much of my life was spent working for the government.

I feel really blessed to be able to have a second career doing work that I love. I am fulfilled with my current life, and I find a certain amount of serenity in working from home. As a matter of fact, "work" is not even an accurate word for what I do.

One of my memories about the places where I worked was that there were very few people who liked their jobs. The last federal building in which I was employed housed over 5,000 employees. The majority of these people were unhappy coming to work every day. Thinking about all of the people I knew, it eventually became obvious to me that most people do not really enjoy their employment, whether they work for the federal government or not.

Of course, there are many reasons why more people are not enjoying their chosen occupations. Quite frankly, most people are working only to get money so that they can acquire basic necessities and survive. I know that was a primary motivation for *my* staying with the government for twenty-seven years. Although the employees were getting paid, most were just so apathetic and unhappy. It seemed as though they had just resigned to their "fate" of being there and not even really grateful for having a job to go to.

As I looked closer at this, I think one of the main sources of unhappiness resulted from relationships between the people—the co-workers, the supervisors, and the friends at the workplace—not the actual work itself. Of course, there were complaints of too much work, not enough work, no meaningful work, and just not liking the work. But, these complaints about the work were secondary to the complaints about the people with whom the majority of our waking hours were spent. The work sites were often akin to being in one, large, and all too often, dysfunctional family.

The problems ranged from someone not recognizing some employees' accomplishments, not giving someone a promotion, or an award, or a special assignment, or vacation time. Or, on a more personal level, there were times when someone did not like another person's race, clothes, hair, or their relationship with some other employee. I have even heard people complain that some employees got new computers, chairs, and even trashcans and that they had not received one.

During my early years of employment at the last department where I worked, I recall many hours where fellow employees would come to my office to complain about their supervisors and their co-workers and they talked about how much they disliked various co-workers. I was not in a position to officially make any change for them or make their situations any better. All I could do was listen to them and sometimes suggest a course of action. Most times, I tried to be positive, and I guess that, coupled with the fact that I listened, encouraged them to come back day after day. Eventually, I had to start closing my office door in order to get my work done. And, I was one of the few employees who enjoyed my work!

I worked for that department for nineteen years. To be fair, I remember some instances where I went to my friends to tell my own stories of discontentment, disbelief, and disappointment with the way things were being done. So I understand the urge to handle things this way. What I eventually realized over the years, though, was that this complaining to one another really got us nowhere. We were not happier after complaining and little was changing for the better in our work environment.

During the last eight years of my career with the government, I learned that what was needed to bring peace and joy to the work site was a change in consciousness. I learned that I had, within myself, all of the tools I needed to master the relationship issues I was experiencing at my workplace. Once I understood that fact, I had no more anxiety from dealing with my co-workers and supervisors.

Relationships are the glue that cements life on this planet. In relationships things are always "relative." Of course, we cannot force anyone to change his or her actions, way of being, or their perception of us or of our work. We do have the power, however, to change our perspective of the things happening to and around us. We also have the power to act on our own behalf. As I began to see situations differently, I found that my situation remarkably changed. Just as we change the channels on our radios and televisions to receive different reception and programming, we can change the "channel" of our relationships by beginning to view them in a different light. We then begin to view and experience a different relationship "program. We have the power to create something else, another experience, in our lives. I learned that it was not the people that were causing me to suffer; I was causing myself suffering.

If you have a problem with work relationships, perhaps the following steps I took may be helpful to you.

1. Recognize that you are dissatisfied. Realize that you do not want to continue relating to the people around you as you have been relating to them in the past because it causes too much distress in your life. Say to yourself that you no longer choose these situations. Announcing this to yourself indicates a shift in consciousness and leads to a shift in your environment. Pray for strength and guidance and pray for the people that you are dealing with.

2. Stop talking negatively about your situation or the people with whom you must interact. The spoken word feeds energy into what you already have decided you no longer want in your life. If people are coming to you with negative dialogue, it may be challenging, but you have the right to say, "I just do not want to discuss this with you anymore." Better yet, you can start interjecting positive, affirmative statements about the situation. There are always some aspects of good in every situation. I found this point to be extremely powerful. Either, the people started seeing the positive that I was speaking of, or they just stopped talking to me about things. To create the good, we can verbally affirm the good.

3. Realize that people will begin to react differently to you, and accept this as part of the process that leads to more positive relationships and environments. As your consciousness changes, you will begin to feel and act differently. Some people will not want to associate with you, and this could initially be a little bit disconcerting, but this is fine because it is evidence that the process you have begun is *working*. What these people think of you is really not your concern. Keep affirming the good that is increasingly present in your life.

4. As it becomes quieter in your environment, peace and serenity will begin to envelop you. You will begin to connect with the divine within and outside of yourself. This is a wonderful place. You are no longer anxious or

tired. You do your own tasks much better and with more clarity. You are walking in the light, and frequently people who can help you, offer to give you help. Opportunities for growth and advancement become more apparent.

5. Express gratitude for the wonderful changes that are taking place. More appropriate assignments and better relationships develop for you. I actually had people offering to give me better jobs, award money, and better assignments. This was the point of real amazement for me because I was not aware, before I changed my consciousness, that all of these wonderful results were forthcoming. I was so grateful to God for the newfound good in my life.

Hopefully, this message will be helpful to you. Something has compelled me to write about this experience. Moreover, I know that the process I put forth works for bettering our personal relationships as well as our professional relationships. Even after we have retired from our primary professions, we are still involved with people on a personal level and in other organizations and groups to which we belong. No matter what type of relationships we are experiencing, we can use them for our spiritual growth and become stronger in spirit. As we move spiritually to a higher level, we begin to see the manifestation of this growth in every experience we have. Remember, God loves us all and is the *One* of which we are all a part. God desires only the best relationships for all of us.

Chapter 17
Choose Love While On Your Inner Space Odyssey

In December 2000 when the year 2001 was just about to make its appearance, I began thinking of an old movie entitled *2001: A Space Odyssey*. Although released back in 1968, perhaps some of you remember this film. I remember going to see it on a date with my boyfriend, and I did not like it at all. The film seemed to be so cold, masculine, and preposterous. In addition, I remember it as being extremely long—making matters worse, in my opinion. At that time, I could not even imagine any of us getting to the year 2001. Needless to say, I certainly could not imagine myself on any "space odyssey" to outer space. I remember sitting there and wondering where was the relevance of this film to *my* life.

Even though I could not envision it at the time, I now realize that I have been on a space odyssey. This has not been a journey into *outer* space, of course, but one into *inner* space. I dare say that most of us have taken, and are still on, this journey. Everything happens in space and time; nothing remains static.

If you look at yourself on the inside, at your inner self, you will agree that you too have been on this journey. Ask yourself the following questions.

1. Are you holding the exact religious or spiritual beliefs that you held when you were, say, nineteen years old?
2. Are you reacting to situations with the same emotions that you felt when you were nineteen years old?
3. Are you holding the same moral ideas that you held when you were nineteen years old?

Most of you probably answered "no" to these questions. I know that I did. Answering in the negative indicates to me that I have indeed been traveling on a journey —my own personal *Inner Space Odyssey*. Most likely you have been on one, too. This inner space odyssey has been one of spiritual transformation and, hopefully, spiritual growth. The real question is what have we learned on our journey?

One predominate lesson I am learning to understand is that *love is all*. If we have learned to love ourselves as we were created without wishing we looked different, had a different upbringing, or had this or that material possession, then we have traveled far. If we have learned to love each cell in our bodies, then we have traveled far.

If we have learned to love our friends and family even though they do not behave as we do, then we have traveled far. Further, if we have learned that there is not room for judgment or negative criticism when love presides, then our friends and families become the variety and spice in a life journey that is purposeful and joyful.

If we have learned to love our past experiences, whether we consider them good or bad, as they are the basis of who we are now, our journey has become brighter and more exciting. Although we can do nothing to change the past, the past is our foundation for the present and has truly gotten each of us to where we are now. We can bless each past experience for helping to shape us into who we are now.

Most importantly—God, the Creator of all, resides in Inner Space. God is love and love is all. Hopefully, we are all learning this while we travel in our own personal space and individual time.

Chapter 18
Cherish The Moments With Your Family

This morning I woke up facing a photograph which brought back a flood of memories into my life. While staring at the picture, I feel as though I am transported back to the very moment of the scene, as if the events the camera has captured are taking place right now at this very moment.

The photograph shows my grandmother, mother, and daughter standing together with arms linked, outside of my daughter's college campus apartment building. The description of the scene may sound pretty simple, but there is such beauty and emotion in this picture. Each of them is projecting an inner joy of being right where they were at the time. Their faces are beaming. I can remember the day so clearly. I, too, am a part of the scene, as the photographer.

We were there to see my daughter, Carla, receiving a scholastic award. My grandmother had never seen the campus and my mother wanted to support and to congratulate Carla and keep me company while driving on the road.

In the photo, Carla is standing between them and she seems to represent a connection between generations. She stands as an embodiment and realization of the principles and dreams that my grandmother and mother had dreamed for her, for me, and for all of the children in the family. I can vividly recall who each of these women were at various stages of their lives and who they were in every stage of my life. We pass so much on to our children, grandchildren, and parents. Even though we may not consciously educate them, we sometimes pass our knowledge on through the fact that we are living together in the same place and space in time. Although we all have distinct personalities, as a family we are indeed one – from generation to generation.

Here we are representing four generations. We were two grandmothers, four daughters, and two granddaughters -- from 20 years old to 86 years old. Each of us is trying to do our best to support one another, each of us finding a special connection and unique closeness with the other.

I look back on these road trips to the University of Maryland Eastern Shore with special fondness. The six-and-a-half hour roundtrip in the car, talking about matters close to our hearts, always resulted in a closer bond between me and whoever was my traveling companion. When Carla and I were alone on the drive there and back, we would have a fantastic time stopping to get donuts and singing to taped music. Whenever we rented a van to haul her stuff back, we really liked riding up above the other cars.

I really appreciated how precious that time was, and relished it, because I remembered previously enjoying riding with my son, Tony, and how that time together seemed to vanish so quickly. He and I would listen to the music of John Coltrane or George Clinton. We analyzed their sounds as well as the issues of the day. He and I would still be talking non-stop when we walked through our door.

Life is, however, a series of continual transitions. Many times these transitions are slow and go almost unnoticed. Whether we pay attention or not, circumstances are continually changing. This photo represents one point in time in my life and in theirs. A time that I was fortunate enough to recognize as precious and just enjoyed it to the hilt! I am grateful for this because, in the past, I had not always recognized and/or paid attention to such meaningful periods.

Carla graduated and moved out of town and Go-Go passed away years ago. Mama and I still hang out together. But the mix of energy and spirit on that particular day can never be re-created. The four of us have transitioned to different positions in our lives and in our family. Mama is now the matriarch of the family, and Carla is a wife, mother, and physician. And me—well, since that photo, I am now a grandmother, and understanding the joy my mother and grandmother felt at the accomplishments of their grandchildren and great-grandchildren.

Life is a continuum—positions shift—chances come around, and move on. But, whatever position we may be in, we must take the time to see, feel, and enjoy what it is like to be right where we are at any particular moment. We must see the value, bless, and be grateful for being in the place that we are, because before we know it—like the click of a camera—the moment will pass on. Keep your moment in focus. Most importantly, don't miss it.

Chapter 19
Develop A Consciousness Of Health

There are many things that we are told are essential to supporting good health: healthy food, clean water, exercise, rest, vitamins, medications, herbal supplements, and avoidance of stress. I certainly believe that all of these things can be beneficial in building and maintaining our physical and emotional health. However, there are times when we are doing many, or all, of these things and still face health challenges. At such times, it may seem strange to us that we are experiencing health problems, especially if we are living what we consider to be a healthy lifestyle.

Our thoughts may be that perhaps we are doing these healthy things in the wrong proportions, or in the wrong combinations. Maybe we are doing too much of one thing, or maybe we are doing too little of another thing. How can we really know since each of us is a unique individual?

Although we may be covering the physical and emotional aspects of our lives that encourage health, we need to build up the spiritual component of our lives. This is where I feel that having what I refer to as a "consciousness of health" comes into play. I define this consciousness as a knowing and understand that, in truth, God has created us as perfect beings, and it is the God within us that sustains this perfection. Perfect health is a component of fully accepting and understanding this perfection.

Realizing this truth can be difficult because we must understand and keep the truth of our perfection in mind at all times, even though physical appearances may cause us to believe otherwise. Living a spiritual consciousness of health requires our engaging our minds and spirits, *as well as* engaging in all of the traditional and non-traditional things we "do" to acquire and maintain health.

To understand this consciousness, we need to first accept and understand the connection of the mind, body, and spirit. Each of us is composed of these inseparable components. Whatever we think in our minds has the ability to be created in our physical world. Our reality should be, in terms of our health, that we *are* healthy.

Living a consciousness of health is a simple answer, in comparison to all of the other things we do to achieve good health, but it is sometimes the most difficult to put into practice. Part of the difficulty is years of programming that being unhealthy is just a part of life. By the time we have reached this point in our lives, we have all experienced some health challenges. When we experienced these challenges, they were very real to us.

In addition, in our society, the media will not allow people to relax and believe in optimal health. There are proliferations of pharmaceutical ads on television, in magazines, and on the Internet. On the other hand, we constantly hear about these "helpful" drugs being recalled and taken off the market. We do not know what to trust.

We repeatedly hear statistics about how many people have various diseases, in addition to disturbing projections of how many others will become sick in the future. These troubling projections and predictions always appear to be more ominous for the African-American community.

With all of this being forced upon us, of course, it is difficult to see the perfection in ourselves. Our minds become saturated with these depressing ideas, and we become stressed and fearful. These ideas become part of our subconscious mind and the community's mass consciousness. And, in recent years, we are being made more and more aware of these pessimistic projections. Although we should pay attention to research findings, we must not absorb this data to the point of becoming fearful and anxious. With all of this occurring, it is hard to maintain a consciousness of perfect health. These are, of course, my feelings about what is happening; perhaps you have other ideas.

My point is, when speaking of the consciousness of health, God lives within each of us and *God is perfect*. We must begin to perceive the God within, and ourselves, as perfect and healthy. We must love our bodies and think and speak positive statements about, and to, our bodies. We can speak health and life into each cell and know that the God within is creating this perfection. We must begin to feel the thrill and vibration of this health and vitality and strive to be joyful.

As we begin to still ourselves, take deep breaths, and to pray, we will begin to know that the mind, the body, and spirit are indeed one. God is one with us and with all things. While feeling this oneness, we can verbally affirm that all is well with us. If we have questions about our health or any other area of our lives, the God within us is waiting to give us the answers. We have only to be still and ask. We remain always thankful for this health that we have. Gratitude to the Creator, and knowing that we are co-creators with God, is essential to success in achieving and maintaining optimal health. If we are praying for the health of others, we must see them as whole, healthy, vibrant and connecting with their God presence.

I realize that putting the idea of this consciousness of health into practice may be demanding, and may not be easy to master. We must let go of years and layers of programming that relate and speak to imperfection as opposed to perfection. However, with practice, just like everything else, it gets easier and easier. Each day, we develop more and more gratitude because each day we get better and better spiritually, emotionally, and physically.

I have tried to relate this to you as best I can. I have experienced the truth in what I am telling you. Health is essential to our being more productive members of our community. Health has been a focus of mine for many years, and I come from a family of healers (and some hypochondriacs) of various disciplines from my great-grandmother to my daughter. They have all shared so much with me. My conclusion is that the mind, the inner person, is directly related to the state of the body, the outer person. A healthy spirit is the foundation to a healthy mind and a healthy body.

Chapter 20
Get Excited About Life

Are you excited about life? Do you approach every new day with anticipation and joy? Hopefully the answer to these questions is a resounding "YES"!

Many of us go through life preoccupied with our responsibilities and our relationships, and are unable to see all of the exciting, glorious life that surrounds us. It is possible for us to feel excitement every day of our lives; and if not every day, then at least most of our days. I am referring to excitement for being a part of the creation and participating in this human experience. This is truly a gift to us, and how we feel about it is a matter of our perspective and consciousness.

I grew up in an immediate family of seven people where I was the oldest child. I have two sisters and two brothers. They are all very talented in their own right and very special. During my childhood, I spent most of my time with my sister, Denise, who is closest to me in age. We were almost always together. We were, as usually is the case with siblings, very different from each other as children. I was a shy, introverted, contemplative child. Denise was an outgoing, sociable, talkative, happy child.

However, in looking back, I can see that she was always excited about everything —no matter how small or seemingly insignificant. I am sure that sometimes her enthusiasm was met by my silence. She seemed to approach and receive everything with excitement! I can hear her now saying, "Oh, Susan, look at that beautiful puppy," or "I know that I have the winning raffle ticket to win that bicycle," or "Feel this kitten, Susan. It is sooo soft." All of this would be said with such exuberance and enthusiasm, that at times I, too, would become excited. I could go on and on telling stories about our childhood dialogues.

Although I may have recognized some of the things from the perspective that she saw them, I was focused more on the world in my head, and the fears that I had. I mean, what if the cute puppy could bite me, or the soft kitten had fleas, or out of 300-plus students in the school, she was going to win?

I can remember some instances, in my shyness, where my hope would be that all this enthusiasm and verbal excitement did not draw attention to the two of us. Whenever I would try to relate some "serious" concern of mine to her, she would come back with some happy/silly/crazy statement that would usually end up making me laugh at her.

I went through my adolescent years still living a great portion of my life in my mind and always praying, praying, praying that these fears I had would not manifest. As you may have guessed, there was very little room in my life for continued, sustained, positive excitement about much of anything. Basically, I guess I felt how could one be completely happily excited when no one knew what was going to happen in the future?

Upon becoming a young adult, I began to notice that I could determine how I felt about things. I began to try to see things differently, and, by conscious design, began to see some of what Denise saw. If I was feeling anxious, I could change that feeling by observing and focusing upon some fascinating aspect of Creation's beauty.

This proved to be a way of bringing excitement as well as joy into my being. The new feeling seemed so natural, and resulted in a more peaceful mind. This peace felt much better than the anxiety of worrying about the future and all my responsibilities. Of course maintaining this peace has proven to be an ongoing process. But, the excitement of life is an ongoing occurrence!

There are *always* aspects of Creation to get excited about—they have always been here; we just have to take the time to observe them. For example, I found that I am sometimes blessed with being able to observe a rainbow, with its many colors, after a storm. As I study it, the vibrations of the colors infuse my being with their beauty and energy. This is so exciting! How can I worry about anything at all when this is happening?

More readily, I can watch cloud formations—watch them move gently across the sky. There are also velvety black crows that sit on the telephone wires, vibrantly red cardinals that are nested in a tree. How does it feel to be velvety or red or feathery? How does it feel to fly? Imagine. What feeling do I get when thinking about the sheer exuberance of a child's laughter? Am I still able to feel the child within me? Realizing that we can be one with the vitality of Creation in such a way increases our excitement about living.

Of course, for me, crystals immediately put me in a state of awe, joy, peace, and excitement. Crystals reemphasize to me that there is more than one way to look at any situation. As I turn a crystal around in my hand, I always see something new that I never noticed before that moment. For me, they represent a microcosm of life. In life, as we turn a situation around to view and review it from a different perspective, there is always a positive aspect in place.

Once we start connecting with the beauty and excitement in our environment, then we begin to experience our connection with the Creator and with Creation. We, too, are creators of our experiences and our reality. As we get more and more excited about this, we begin to feel the love and excitement of the Creator. And, with this connection, how can we feel anything but excitement, enthusiasm, and anticipation at all times.

Chapter 21
Sleep In A Quiet Environment

When I was a teenager, I spent many hours watching television. I remember one occasion where my sister and I were watching television in her bedroom and I fell asleep. I had the most vivid dream, woke up, and began telling my sister about the dream. To my surprise, it turned out that I was relating the exact story line of the movie she had just seen and I had slept through. I was amazed because, of course, I did not "see" the movie.

I never forgot this event. In fact, I still remember what the movie was about to this day. Apparently, the subconscious mind has the ability to absorb the audible information that is present in our environment while we are sleeping.

Sleep is a restorative process that serves to replenish the body psychologically and physiologically. Sleep is an essential part of our daily lives. It is very important to each person's state of health.

Noise, in the form of electronic media such as the television and radio, has very definite effects on our state of mind and our psychological health. Recently, I fell asleep while watching a television program, and woke up a couple hours later feeling distressed and fearful. Although I did not remember any particular dialogue, as I had done when "dreaming" the movie as a teenager, I had the bad feelings from the energy of the dialogue and contents of the program.

It turned out that the program was an investigative crime show. The dialogue in the story involved some sordid details and violent behavior. I felt so strange that I jumped up and could not turn the television off fast enough. This experience distressed me. Since I have been falling asleep on television shows for years, there is no telling what type of information has been programmed into my brain, in addition to each cell of my body. Maybe it is not coincidental that these television shows are referred to as television "programs."

On the other hand, I get magazines through the mail that advertise tapes and CDs that promise to alter our behavior and habits. They claim that if you buy and use the tape, you can produce desirable behaviors such as: lose weight, stop smoking, and attain serenity, among many others. This indicates that if these audible suggestions can work while we are asleep or in a relaxed state, then any audible information has an effect on our psyche while we are asleep.

We must pay attention to, and take note of, the type of information that is being put into our minds. We are constantly being bombarded with information and ideas from the Internet, newspapers, radio, television, and the society as a whole. Many times we cannot avoid being affected, but at night, when we should be sleeping, resting, and giving our bodies an opportunity to regenerate, we can create a peaceful space and a quiet environment in which to rest. Our minds are vulnerable to disturbing sounds and information when we are sleeping as well as the period of time just prior to sleep. If you desire a more peaceful and restful sleep, turn off your television. If you find that you are uncomfortable with perfect silence, play some enjoyable, relaxing music and allow it to lull you into a perfect rest. In turn, you will find that your waking hours will be more serene and enjoyable.

Chapter 22
Release The Old And Make Way For The New

Many people have voiced to me their desire to let go of whatever is no longer needed in their lives. In a material way, we may see this as a desire to rid ourselves of clutter. Many of us, including myself, seem to be surrounded by things we have collected that are no longer serving any purpose. My main source of clutter consists of piles of magazines, clippings, and papers that I tell myself that I will need one day. As time goes by, I do not even know what information is contained in this pile of paper, let alone ever have a use for it.

We know that life is cyclical and that letting go of stuff, and sometimes even letting go of relationships, is needed in order to make way for the new. By letting go, we stay in flow with the universe because the universe in which we live is dynamic and ever changing. We should release that which we no longer use in order to make space for the good that is in store for us.

Sometimes we are not holding on to *things* but are holding on to emotional issues. We may carry them with us as if they were part of our physical bodies. Some people collect old hurts, resentments, and injustices, both real and perceived—hanging on to them indefinitely. These negative feelings should be released in order to achieve and maintain emotional and physical health. Negative emotions that are held within become blockages in our energy fields, and can block the energy that flows to our organs and cells. Guess what? These negative emotions manifest themselves, in time, as physical disorders. It is important to examine ourselves periodically to make certain that we are not carrying around old resentments from year to year. Release this heavy baggage, and you will find yourself feeling much lighter and traveling through life in the express lane.

As we move from year to year, are we carrying with us a bunch of physical or emotional clutter? If so, it is time to get rid of it and get a fresh perspective on life. I know it is a difficult task to let go of things, situations, people, and habits with which we have become comfortable. I must constantly revisit throwing away, or giving away, things that clutter up my space. It is hard for me to get started. I find that I can look at the "thing," feel the emotion attached to it, bless it, and let go. Once I begin, the releasing seems to gain momentum and it becomes less painful, and eventually freeing.

We must remember that so much good awaits us. We only have to clear a space for it in our consciousness, and then in our environments and our hearts. The universe is unlimited, so as we bless and let go of what is no longer utilized or needed, we can expect to attract better things and situations into our lives—those that will lead to our highest good.

Chapter 23
Make Time For Fun In Your Life

Most of the topics I have written about will hopefully help build our spirituality and make us better able to deal with life's issues. These topics tend to be serious in nature and require some soul searching and perhaps a little inner work. But in the midst of addressing all of the serious issues confronting us personally, as well as those confronting us communally, there should be some time for us to step aside and just enjoy life. I believe that in order to successfully maneuver through life's challenges and to create the needed balance in our lives, some of our time must be dedicated to having fun.

"Fun" is a word that is not used too much these days. What is "fun"? There are probably as many answers to that question as there are people in existence. In the *New Webster's Dictionary*, "fun" is defined as "pleasure, amusement, and playfulness." I think of fun as anything that brings enjoyment into life. While we are here on earth, we should be enjoying ourselves. Spiritual principles are essential to living a fully conscious and contributory life. I have found that prayer and meditation definitely lead to joy and peace. However, I ask myself, "What are the things that make me laugh and giggle?" Whatever the answer happens to be for each of us, these are the things that we should, especially during this demanding time in history, resurrect and accelerate.

There are countless fun opportunities available to us in life. Our lives need a balance of seriously taking care of our physical and spiritual responsibilities and of seriously seeking enjoyable moments. Are we taking time to engage in fun activities— those things that make us smile and may even seem a little frivolous?

Fun activities can help to relieve stress, and we know that every segment of society that speaks on health tells us that excess stress causes problems for us emotionally and physically. Dancing, playing physical sports, and exercising are some examples of ways to relieve stress and have fun at the same time. The Creator gave us bodies as well as spirits and we should use them. It is essential to our health that we do so. Usually, after engaging in physical activities, we feel peaceful and calm. We have a feeling of wellness that is an additional reward to having fun.

Creative activities and hobbies can be fun for us and also bring enjoyment to others. Drawing, painting, decorating, playing music, writing, and sewing are some examples of creative pursuits that can provide hours of fun. I am blessed to have many friends and family members who are extremely creative. The results of their creativity have provided unending beauty and inspiration to my life. I have been a creative person since childhood, so creative fun is very close to my heart. I have spent countless hours doing artistic things and have been blessed to enjoy every second. We are all born with the gift of creativity. If you are not using your particular gift, you are missing out on experiencing some real fun.

Spending time with friends and family can also be a vehicle to positively reconnect with our human side and have fun at the same time. Taking time out to share a meal with friends affords us an opportunity to be in a new environment and share our life experiences as well. These fun times often give us insight into ourselves as well as others. Many times, the things that we experienced, which may seem exasperating, can end up being somewhat humorous when we relate these events and feelings to someone else. Oftentimes, my friends and —I end up laughing at situations, which initially seemed frustrating and troubling until we spoke about it. Frequently, I have found myself still smiling about some of our conversations weeks after our getting together. My friends usually lend another perspective to my situations that I had been unable to see.

Even if you do not want to talk about your experiences with friends, you can go to see a movie, play, or concert with them and discuss what you saw. During that time, you are temporarily removed from your particular troubles and can focus on other facets of life. It can be even more fun to take a trip with your friends. I have taken trips, even for a day, with friends where our destination was a peaceful, educational, or fun place. But the most fun came in talking for hours while traveling, and from stopping to get fun things to eat along the way regardless of what our destination turned out to be.

I will be the first person to tell you that these are very serious times in which we live and we are seeing many changes take place. To some, this period could prove somewhat unsettling. On the other hand, we must find light moments in which we can revel in order to counter any feelings of tension or gloom. Fun moments can provide the undercurrent upon which we can continually and successfully move into the next serious moment. Fun moments, strung together, allow us to realize a lifetime of joy.

Chapter 24
Non-Judgment Brings Peace

"Peace on earth and good will towards men." I have heard this phrase associated with the Christmas season as far back as I can remember. As I child I wondered if this included women too. Now I wonder what does it mean to have peace on earth. Externally, there are wars and crime, as internally we see people with depression, fear, and anxiety. There is a lack of peace on earth. I, and many others, frequently have to affirm to ourselves "Peace, be still," or "Be still and know that I am God" in order to bring about our own internal balance.

What does it mean to have peace on earth? In my opinion, we must first start achieving our own internal peace. If individually we cannot find peace, I don't see how we can hope to attain a collective peace on earth. Throughout my life, I have tried many approaches to achieving peace of mind and spirit, some of which have pushed me forward. I suppose you have also.

Although there are myriad approaches to achieving that most desired peaceful state, there are two that I have found helpful in my quest for personal peace. One is being able to be still, or silent, which involves setting aside time daily to experience silence. We touched upon this in past newsletters, especially when we addressed meditation. We can decide to be silent during the day for a certain period of time. Periods of meditative silence usher in mental and spiritual peace that results in benefits to our entire day.

The other idea is a little bit different: practice non-judgment. Judgment is the constant evaluation of things as right or wrong, good or bad. Non-judgment means to stop judging every experience that comes along. I have tried this, and it works!! All right, I admit that it is difficult to do because we have been brought up in a society, which teaches us to dissect, analyze, and judge everything in life. However, the analyzing and judging creates a constant internal dialogue in our minds and contributes to our lack of peace. Consider these mental phrases as examples of some of the judgments that can run rampant through the mind: "It is a dreary day," "That's a stupid response," "She's a selfish woman," or "That outfit is tacky." In such cases, we are placing value judgment on what we observe rather than just observing what "is." We could simply view this as another day of life, or merely observe the color of the outfit, or understand that the response we hear is just a matter of opinion, without attempting to judge these things. Wars have been created based upon judgments about people, countries, or what we should or should not have said.

I have not yet gotten to the point of being able to practice non-judgment for days on end because it truly takes practice to free the mind of this internal dialogue for long periods of time. Actually, once you try it, you will see that the act of non-judgment creates silence and peace in the mind.

Try this exercise. Get up in the morning and tell yourself, "I will not judge anything today," and try to stick to this statement. If you find that you are judging during the day, remind yourself of your morning commitment not to judge. You may want to start out with a shorter period of time, perhaps not commit to the whole day, but rather commit to a few hours of non-judgment. When I can do this, I am shocked at the peacefulness of mind that I am able to achieve. The internal chatter quiets down and I realize that I have no authority to judge what the Creator has put here. This judging is a function of my ego and its attempt to determine reality as I see it. But, how is this helping the universe? The practice of non-judgment also allows me to begin to have a more spiritual appreciation for my surroundings and more importantly, for those fellow beings with which I come in contact.

This is a perfect time to practice achieving peace in the world. We must always begin our work internally before we can make changes outside of ourselves. If each of us would try to create this peace through the practice of non-judgment, perhaps we will begin to see peace in the world around us. Remember we *are* this world.

Chapter 25
Aromatherapy Is The Creator's Fragrant Pharmacy

Each year as spring appears, I cannot help but marvel at the greening of the Earth. Trees that sported bare branches and lawns that were tan, brown, or bare are now vibrantly green! With the life that has awakened in the Earth, we all begin to feel life's energy. We feel more vibrant ourselves as the beauty and abundance of nature increases as the days grow longer.

The colorful blossoms appearing everywhere enhance this green color. Many of them are filling the air with heavenly fragrances. Again, we fully awaken to the cyclical wonders of nature, and we feel much more alive. Becoming entranced with the plant kingdom and contemplating its wonders is a perfect time to discuss one of God's special gifts from the plant kingdom: aromatherapy.

In my newsletter, "Living In The Light," I have discussed the benefits of plants and herbs in each issue. Many have shared my excitement in knowing that the Creator is giving us an infinite amount of support and health through plants. Years ago, even before I began studying herbal healing, I remember a friend telling me that she believed God had provided us a cure to every ailment on Earth within nature itself. I remember thinking that this was a comforting idea and quickly got a vision of some remote rainforest filled with unidentified plants. Well, I am now certain that cures abound within the plant kingdom for almost all of our illnesses.

We are discovering, seemingly daily, the specific positive effects that plants are having on our minds, bodies, and spirits. Just look at the rise in production and sale of herbal products in the past fifteen years. This increased consumption of herbs and plant extracts gives testimony to their effectiveness.

Aromatherapy is the use of essential oils that have been extracted from plants, to assist in health and healing. Essential oils are high-grade fuel from plants, and when we use them, we are taking in the best that plants can give us. The oils are described as the plant's life force.

Aromatherapy, like herbal healing, is a part of these "Plant Blessings" from the plant kingdom. It is an ancient healing method that has been revived and is astoundingly growing in popularity today. It has been called the "fragrant pharmacy." It is through the sense of smell and inhalation that much of the essential oils are absorbed into our system. In addition, the oils can be applied externally, to our skin, and they are absorbed through the skin.

There are about 300 essential oils, many of which have one or more of the following properties: antiviral, antibacterial, antifungal, anti-inflammatory, anti-toxic, anti-depressant, antiseptic, sedative, analgesic, and digestive diuretic, to name a few. Essential oils effectively enter and leave the body very quickly. With few rare exceptions, essential oils are non-toxic. Unlike chemical drugs, essential oils are not known to stay in the body. They are released from the body from between six to fourteen hours depending upon the health of the body. The healthier the body, the more quickly they are released. Essential oils can be used in conjunction with other therapies and treatments.

The use of essential oils is an ancient practice. According to the book, *Aromatherapy: A Complete Guide to the Healing Art,* the Egyptians were already using large quantities of myrrh as early as 3000 BC. Papyrus manuscripts reveal that Egyptians utilized fragrant herbs, oils, perfumes, and temple incense, as well as healing salves made with fragrant resins. Egyptian aromas were extremely powerful. Even after thousands of years, a slight odor of frankincense was noticeable when King Tutankhamen's tomb was opened. From that time, we find historical references to use of essential oils in China, in the Old Testament, and in ancient Greece.

Native Americans have historically burned incense and utilized scented ointments. The Aztecs and the Incas prepared scented healing salves and herbal ointments for massages. Traditionally, Native Americans smudged sick people with smoke from fragrant herbs. Smudge sticks of cedar and sage are still used, to this day, in order to purify people and the environment.

In the Old Testament, God directed Moses to make holy anointing oil from "flowing myrrh, sweet cinnamon, calamus, cassia, and olive oil." This formula results in a powerful antiviral and antibiotic substance for protection from, and treatment of, illnesses.

Some of the ways in which we can use essential oils are as follows:

1. Inhaling Oils from Tissues – Add one drop of oil to a tissue and inhale the scent.
2. Inhale Vapors from the Oils – Add oil to a bowl of hot water and inhale directly or from the vapors that have dispersed into the environment.
3. Massage Oil – Use about five drops of essential oil to a teaspoon of vegetable oil. Massage this into the body.
4. In Baths – Add about eight drops to bath water.

5. With Candles – Add one to two drops of oil to warm melted candle wax.
6. With Diffusers – Add one to six drops of essential oil to the diffuser.
7. Room Sprays – Add four or more drops of essential oil to a cup of water. Pour into a plant sprayer and spray mixture into the room.
8. Create Water Bowls – Add one to nine drops of oil in a bowl of boiling water.

There are other methods, but these are the ones that I have used and can attest to their effectiveness. *The Complete Book Of Essential Oils & Aromatherapy* by Valerie Ann Worwood gives more detailed information on these and other methods of using essential oils.

What are some of the plant essences that are used for aromatherapy? The names are almost as numerous as the number of plant species. Some are common, such as lemon, cinnamon, and rose. Others are less well known such as spikenard (which is referred to in the Bible), mimosa, and hyssop. Needless to say, the catalog of oils is too voluminous to discuss here, as there are said to be over 300 essential oils.

To give you a little idea about what the oils can do for you, I have listed examples of a few of the commonly used oils and their effects.

***Lavender**. Lavender is known as the universal oil. It aids sleep, soothes tired muscles, benefits the immune system, and encourages stillness and tranquility. It is good for burns, rashes, psoriasis, and may help with insomnia, vaginal infections, and cystitis. I have used lavender oil more often than any other oil. I use it primarily to create a relaxing atmosphere in my house. It smells divine.

***Eucalyptus**. Eucalyptus is a wonderful, stimulating oil, especially during the winter months. It is a powerful, penetrating bactericidal and antiviral oil for sickrooms. It is good for sinus problems, herpes, and chicken pox. It is an excellent decongestant, and relieves stiffness when applied to the body. I use eucalyptus to open up my sinuses.

*__Frankincense__. Frankincense aids meditation, prayer, and it fortifies and quiets the mind. It encourages feelings of health and wellness. It was well known for its healing powers during the time of Christ and has been used extensively in Egypt. One of my favorite childhood memories is of frankincense wafting through the Catholic church that I attended. It is anti-catarrhal, anti-tumor, immune stimulating, and anti-depressant. I use frankincense to reinforce positive vibrations in my space.

If you want to become more acquainted with aromatherapy, which is an excellent alternative healing choice, I suggest you read a book on aromatherapy. I found *Aromatherapy: A Complete Guide to the Healing Art* by Kathi Keville and Mindy Green to be one of the best resources on the history of aromatherapy and for helping one to determine which oils, methods, and formulas are most suitable for a specific purpose.

Chapter 26
Create Happiness In Your Life

When my youngest sister, Rhonda, was a small girl, she was a happy child, but she was rather grumpy in the mornings. She did not like to get out of bed. She had a hard time saying, "Good morning," when we greeted her at the breakfast table each morning. My grandmother noticed Rhonda's attitude and gave Rhonda a printed Bible verse to stick on her dresser mirror, so that Rhonda could see this each and every day. It read, "This is the day that the Lord has made. Let us rejoice and be glad in it."

I don't know about Rhonda, but this really impressed me. I remember going into Rhonda's bedroom, looking in the mirror, and wondering if this would make her more joyful in the morning. I cannot remember there being too much change, if any, in Rhonda's attitude, but then, she was only about seven years old.

Recently, I attended a church service with my mother, and was surprised when the congregation began singing, "This is the day that the Lord has made…" The verse had been put to music, and it was melodiously repeated over and over again. As I joined in the singing, I began to feel happy. The tune chosen for the verse was catchy, joyful, and upbeat.   It seemed that the more I sang, the happier I became, and the more exuberantly I sang. Memories of

Rhonda and my grandmother came flooding back into my mind. I was happy that my grandmother had given the verse and realized that it was as much a legacy to me as it was to Rhonda.

At the end of 2001, I began feeling an intensity of energy around me unlike I had felt at any other time. Most of my close friends and family were experiencing some intense issue or lesson. Perhaps this intense energy or heaviness was resultant from the September 11 events surrounding the World Trade Center catastrophe. Things just seemed so heavy, and my peoples' health, security, relationships, and even sanity were being challenged. I knew that although I was generally happy, I wanted and needed to experience more joy in my life. My analytical, thinking side wondered what I could do to increase this joy … and this led to the question "What is joy?"

Right after New Year's Day 2002, I visited my daughter in Manhattan. I love the city, but was a little apprehensive about going there after the effects of the World Trade Center/ September 11 events on the atmosphere there. I was looking forward to seeing my daughter and her husband, but wondered if this was going to be another heavy, intense experience. I prayed on the train ride to New York that we would have a joyful visit.

To my surprise, people were acting the same way they had the last time I was there several months earlier. They were going about their business as usual. They were pleasant. I experienced more people on the street greeting me and smiling at me than I experienced at home in Washington. Moreover, these people had experienced September 11 in a more horrible way than me. I realized that God has given all of us an innate resilience that we can call upon to return to happiness and joy even after experiencing trauma. Contrary to the concerns I may have felt, I was very joy-filled there and began to feel myself returning to a "lightness of being."

My daughter, son-in-law, and I were all so happy. We were laughing, talking, walking for hours, and saying silly things to encourage our laughter. I sensed within my body and spirit that a real change was taking place. My energy level increased exponentially, and the tension I felt before arriving in the city had vanished.

I remember that upon my arrival, my spirits immediately changed. I was the same person—the only difference was a train ride and visiting with loved ones. The joy was always there; I had to be conscious of it and perceive, grasp, and hold on to it.

I realized that joy and happiness are always available; they are always here. With God, we can create the joy and happiness that we desire. Joy and happiness can be experienced right here, right now, if we accept it. These attitudes really come from within—they are part of the God presence that we all possess. We access joy and happiness by knowing and accepting the God within and communicating with our God within. Perhaps this is one reason why just receiving the Bible verse did not really make Rhonda happy to get up in the morning. Being a little girl, she needed to be able to "feel the message," not just read the message.

Some years ago, I read a book entitled *The Art of Happiness*, by His Holiness The Dalai Lama and Howard Cutler who is an American psychiatrist. One of the most impressive statements in the book was "whether we are feeling happy or unhappy at any given moment often has very little to do with our absolute conditions, but rather it is a function of how we perceive our situation, how satisfied we are with what we have." Happiness has to do with our perceptions.

Happiness can be experienced in waking up in the morning—waking into another day of life and opportunity. The sun is again streaming in the window and the birds are singing. Natural occurrences such as these seem to inspire happiness. Happiness and joy can be experienced in hearing the voice of a child or seeing the smile of a child. Knowing that we are blessed with food and shelter, when many of our brothers and sisters are hungry and homeless, should spark happiness and gratitude within us. When I ponder these things that make me happy and joyful, I can feel the atoms of my body dancing with delight.

Even when our situations seem challenging, we can bring about joy by looking for, and finding the good, in our situations. And, there is always some good to be found. Along with pondering the positive side of our challenges, we should also visualize and anticipate a positive outworking of our challenges.

Happiness and laughter raise the vibration in our bodies and our energy fields and this promotes health and wellness. Happiness is essential to our well being and creates light energy. Remember, there have been scientific studies and resultant evidence as to the healing power of laughter.

When looking at small children, we often see how effortlessly joyful they can be. Perhaps we can take cues from them and not take others and ourselves so seriously. When situations occur which throw us off balance, and out of joy, we can begin to just let them roll away from us and return to our rightful state of happiness and joy. Forgiveness of people and situations is a great help in this area.

If we have experienced trauma in our lives, we may need help in grasping the happiness and joy that is within us. There are some things we can do to stimulate our re-awakening to our joy: listen to music that makes us feel happy; invest time in a hobby we enjoy; do a kind deed for someone in need; find humor in daily occurrences; smile and greet people as we encounter them; experience the delightful fragrances of flowers, essential oils, or foods; sing a song, especially upon awakening; dance around our homes; pray for joy; affirm that we are experiencing unspeakable joy; and live with a sense of gratitude.

As we continue to do the things that bring us happiness and joy, we will begin to embody and express this happy, joyful attitude to those we meet. Just think, we can be powerful agents in the uplifting of others. If all of us can do this, we will raise our own vibrations, and as we are all one, the vibrations of those around us will be raised as well. I am committed to experiencing and sharing more happiness and joy. Won't you join me?

Chapter 27
Loneliness vs. Solitude

Most of us have experienced being alone at some time or another. When we are alone, do we feel lonely or do we enjoy the solitude? As a child I felt that the jazz standard, "Solitude" made being alone seem sad and haunting. (It is a great tune though!) But now, I unemotionally see solitude as simply being by oneself without the company of others. Thus for me, solitude does not necessarily mean being lonely. It is not sad and does not have the negative connotation that loneliness has.

There have been times when I was living with family members, not being alone, and I felt lonely. On the other hand, there was a time when I was in the house, by myself, and neither felt alone nor lonely. It seemed to me that God, angels, and ancestors were surrounding me at all times.

As a child, I grew up in a family of seven. I was never alone, and I never remember our house being quiet, except at night when everyone was asleep. I remember hiding out in the bathroom just to be away in a quiet space.

Leaving my parents' home at age twenty to get married, I discovered that I had an aversion to being alone. I was accustomed to having family or friends around me at all times. That was all I knew, and that situation seemed crucial to my emotional health.

I can recall feeling so terrifyingly lonely when I first got married because my husband worked in a hospital on the night shift. Once we had children, I never had to be alone again.

When the children left, I started living alone. By then, I was forty-six and had never lived alone. I learned that being alone may be jolting in the beginning, but solitude afforded me the opportunity to get in touch with "me." I began to hear myself speak internally and I heard my answers and responses to my own "self questioning."

Now, as an older adult, my spirit cries for segments of time where I have solitude. It is as essential to me as having air to breathe. I went from someone who hated being alone in early adulthood to one who cherishes each minute of solitude. In those precious minutes are countless opportunities to be with the God who lives within us (and outside of us) in this wonderful universe.

Looking back at my life, it all seems rather odd now. When my children were young and I worked downtown, the only time I had any solitude was when I walked or ate alone on my lunch hour.

I think creative people understand more than others the need for solitude. It is then that we can channel God's energy through us into whatever we create. The primary point to remember is that it seems as though we spiritually took on this life *by ourselves* and we will spiritually complete it by ourselves. However, we are always with God; *we are never alone.* This is one of the most comforting, profound understandings we can acquire. Once understood, we find joy whether alone or in the company of others.

To have time for solitude is a gift that can allow us to grow spiritually. Having loving family and friends to spend time with also is a gift. The best gift of all is in knowing how to balance these two gifts to better serve our lives and the lives of others.

Chapter 28
God Is Energy

When I watch my grandchildren, I notice that they exhibit boundless energy. They run, jump, and roll on the ground without thought of possible injuries. Sometimes they do get hurt, but this does not prevent them from getting up and continuing to run, jump, and roll on the ground.

Sometimes I play games with them that require abundant physical energy. They invariably want to go on and on, but I give out long before they want to stop the games. In the deep recesses of my memory, I vaguely see myself, years ago, energized to the extent that they are now.

When most adults are asked how they feel, they frequently answer that they are tired. Of course, we have been here on Earth doing things much longer than the children. As we grow older, we just do not have the time, inclination, or energy level to keep up with a child of four-, five-, or six- years old. It makes sense that because our bodies are not as youthful as theirs, our energy level is not as great. However, we are still alive so we can and should move our bodies as much as possible, even if we are moving slowly and more deliberately.

How are we going to move through our day as enthusiastically and energetically as children? Just like the children, we too are infused with God's energy, and our access to energy is unlimited. We can start our day in the following way. When we wake up in the morning, we can affirm and envision God's energy as light running through our veins into every cell of our bodies, a light that will help us accomplish whatever we need to do whether it be getting out of our beds, playing tennis, or walking up a staircase.

Just as we envision this energy as light moving through our bodies and enhancing us physically, we can also see this light *healing* any physical problem we may have. This light can move through the cells of our bodies and create spiritual and emotional well being, too. The energy that flows to us from God is life enhancing, unlimited in supply, and life sustaining.

As we see this energy flow through every cell of our body, we know that it cannot help but flow out from us and permeate our surroundings and those around us. By envisioning and connecting with this energy that flows through the cells of our bodies, we feel more energetic and alive. With enthusiasm, we are ready to face the challenges and rewards of our day with the same expectancy and anticipation of children.

Chapter 29
The Healing Process

In 2001, I took a self-imposed leave of absence from writing my newsletter. In May of that year, after getting several mammograms, and subsequent biopsy, I was shocked when my doctor told me that the biopsy indicated the presence of some cancer cells. I had surgery (a lumpectomy) to remove some tissue. The surgery was a one-day, in/out surgery. Afterward, I chose to have radiation therapy, and I was blessed that my situation was non-invasive. Through the power of God's grace, love, and light, and the prayers of many, I healed and am in perfect health!

This was a life-transforming experience for me. I learned many things, and had an opportunity to better use my faith. Through this experience, I was given another opportunity to practice many of the principles that I so often read and talk about.

One night, I began writing down the steps or process that I took myself through in order to turn my health challenge into a positive experience. I see that many people are experiencing fear and turmoil at this time, due not only to disease, financial problems, and other personal challenges, but also as a result of critical events that are occurring on the world stage. One of the significant events which challenged the public's peace of mind during the time I was going through my personal healing process was the September 11, Twin Towers tragedy. It occurred to me that the following steps I took to turn my health challenge around could assist others who are facing their own challenges. Through this process, I came to know what "living in the light" really means to me. The following is my process.

Be still. Quiet your mind. Still your body. Take time to be quiet. Cancel appointments and ignore phone calls, if necessary. You must discipline your spirit and you must focus. Once the body and mind become still, the presence of God becomes very obvious. God, who lives within (and without), is forever waiting for us to be in contact with the God presence. God desires to assist us with all of our needs, but we must quiet our outer activities (stop or slow down) in order to better hear and feel God's presence and direction.

Make contact with God. Call upon God and affirm God's presence within you. Know that God is always with you and that nothing can separate you from God. You and God are one. God's love and light are available to all of us at all times.

Ask God to help with whatever you need in your life. God wants us to ask. God is unlimited in love and in supply. We have but to ask. I believe that God knows what we need even before we ask. However, when we ask, we are affirming our desire to have what we need. This is important because sometimes we may be unclear as to what our desires are. Pray that *God's* will be done in your life. **Know** that God has already answered your prayer and that although you may not see your desire manifested immediately, it is being answered—it has been done. This is the Truth.

Ask God for clarity and understanding about the particular situation that you are experiencing. What has brought you to this point? What, and how, can you learn from the situation? What does God want you to do about it? How can you use the situation to better serve God? This involves work on a very deep, spiritual level.

Listen for God's answer. This is extremely important. You should practice being aware. During those quiet times, the answer may be heard in that still, small voice within. Look and listen to your environment. The answer could come through the comments of friends or strangers. Pay attention to books or articles that you pick up to read, or especially those that you are given to read—the answer could be staring at you. God's answer could come through some lecture, sermon, or seminar. Be conscious and expectant that the answer is here, so pray to become aware of it and to accept it once you know. Be willing to maintain a period of silence/stillness/meditation each day. This will keep your lines of communication with God open at all times, and free of outside interference.

Be ready and willing to act upon the information you received. You have stilled yourself, you have asked for God's help, God has cleared away the confusion and supplied you with truth, and God has shown you in which direction to go. Now, you must follow through. This is a most important, and sometimes difficult, step. This is because usually some part of your life, or habits, may have to change. You may have to step out into new territory, but this is always a part of growth. You must have faith and trust that the answers you receive from God are for your highest good, no matter how different or unusual they may seem. Be open and receptive to new direction. When we look at the Bible, or the life story of any great person, we see many instances where people are asked to do things way out of the ordinary for them at the time. God protects them and blesses them as they follow divine inspiration and guidance. We must be willing to follow our divine inspirations no matter what others do or think, or what **we** have previously done or thought.

Know that all is well. Trust God to do what is best for you. God is Universal Intelligence. This intelligence is available to all of us. Know that God wants only good for us in every area of our lives. Let go and let God be in control of your life. This can be hard for those who want to have control. We all know that God can do a better job than we do by ourselves. I know that God and I are the majority, and that with God all things are possible. Know and feel this in every cell and fiber of your being.

This can sometimes be difficult because those around you, even some of those close to you, may challenge you as you begin to realize this truth and act in response to this knowledge. Your own mind may want to jump around with thoughts like "what about this," "what if that happens," "how can you be sure," or "who do you think you are?" But, you must quiet these thoughts and peacefully affirm the truth that you are God's child; God is in charge of your life, body, mind, and affairs; and, that all is well!!! Release all fears and doubts. This may not be easy and is a study in and of itself. Fear is very complex, and can be defeating.

Pray without ceasing. What can I say? You just keep praying throughout the day and night. Affirm love, peace, and order in your life. Create your own special affirmation, or take one from a holy book, and just say it whenever you can—and you **can**. When things appear difficult or frustrating, say a prayer. Visualize yourself surrounded by and infused with God's golden light. When you experience the joy and beauty of God's creation or experience peace, say a prayer of gratitude and praise. Through prayer, you will find that you will become refocused, and the peaceful, joyful times will become more frequent.

See the positive and speak the positive. Negativity prevents God's light from shining on and through you. Look for the good in your situation. Good is always there even if you cannot identify it at the time. Visualize yourself in the most perfect condition you desire. Feel the joy of it. If you cannot identify good in the situation you are experiencing, see the good in God's creation. The sun is still shining and enhancing all life. Birds are still singing and soaring high. Flowers are still blooming. Include and experience these wonders in your life. See them, feel them, ponder them, and allow them to wash over you.

Watch the words you speak. Stop referring to yourself in the negative (poor, sick, crazy, tired, etc.). Words are things and are part of you creating your world. You want to create the best for your life. Doing this can be challenging because you may have been making certain negative statements about yourself, or others, for as long as you can remember. Monitor your words and ask yourself if this is the truth you believe, or want to believe, about yourself or others. Begin to say positive things about yourself and others, and you will find that your life will change as you make progress in this area. I am a student of Unity principles, and Unity teaches that we should be particularly careful to follow any statement beginning with "I am …" with *only* positive words or phrases.

Be grateful, be grateful, and be grateful! I cannot emphasize this enough. We all have so much to be thankful for. Even in times of challenge we must be grateful. Express this gratitude to God and to others on your path. Thank God for answering your prayer—immediately after your petition. God hears us and answers us in ways that are always for our highest good. This is such a blessing. Continually give praise to God. By expressing gratitude, you know and God knows "it is done," and you have accepted your good in spirit even though it may not yet have physically materialized. Through gratitude you are expressing faith and trust that God is doing the great work in your life. What more could you ever need?

30 "In-Lightened" Things To Do

1. **FORGIVE** – Extend forgiveness to someone who has offended you. You may offer forgiving words to them or you may say silently, in your heart, "I forgive you." Remember to forgive yourself for any real or perceived mistakes you have made. The act of forgiveness heals the forgiver in mind, spirit, and body.

2. **GIVE YOUR GIFTS TO OTHERS** – It does not matter what the gift is, giving is a way to keep us in flow with the action of the universe. Gifts do not have to be material. Actually, the most precious gifts we can give are those of our time and attention. There is so much value in the gift of a compliment or a word of encouragement. In God's universe, giving is the same as receiving and represents a circular flow of energy in a universe where nothing is static. In that vein, we should graciously accept all gifts given to us. Remember that all gifts come from God.

3. **STOP SEEKING EXTERNAL APPROVAL** – If we rid ourselves of a need for external approval, we can gain greater freedom and peace. We alone, as individuals, can judge our worth. Many people are shackled by the need for someone else to approve their actions. This need keeps them enslaved to what others think about them or about their actions. As a result, they disturb their own peace.

    There are times when some of us may say, wear, buy, and even think something based upon how we feel others will view us. Our goal in life should be to discover our God-given worth regardless of what anyone else thinks. By relinquishing the need for approval, and ceasing to worry about what others think, we will find that we are able to make substantial progress on our personal spiritual paths.

4. **BE READY TO CHANGE** – Besides the proverbial death and taxes, change is another one of life's certainties. Whether we initiate change or not, *change happens.* Just as the ocean flows in and out daily, and the sand on the beach is reconfigured after each movement of the ocean, our lives are in a constant state of redesign. Many of us fear the unfamiliar, because we feel comfortable with what we know. Ultimately, fear of stepping out into the unknown inhibits our growth. We are constantly faced with new beginnings whether large or small.

    Whether we initiate change or change finds us, we can look at change as an opportunity to grow in another direction and to learn new things. Remember that God never leaves us, and as we take a new direction in life, we can depend on God's love for guidance, support, protection, and comfort.

5. **BRING NATURE INDOORS** – During the fall and winter months, many of us can expect a decrease in daylight hours and cooler temperatures. The greenery and colorful flowers that we enjoyed during the prior months will be gone. We begin to spend more time indoors. Retreating to the indoors, coupled with less sun, warmth, and blooming plants, may cause some of us to feel a little depressed. We can combat these feelings by bringing more of nature into our homes and work environment. Bringing those plants indoors could re-create the outdoor experience. The green color of plants is healing, and their presence helps to cleanse the air.

    Other options are to purchase fresh cut flowers or surround ourselves with pictures of nature, such as seascapes, flowers, sunsets, or our favorite vacation photos to help boost our mood. While looking at these pictures and absorbing the scenes, we can visualize being at one with what is pictured. We can *be* there. Nature allows us to experience God's love by bringing order, beauty, joy, and peace into our lives.

6. **TRUST AND USE YOUR INTUITION** – We all have the gift of intuition. This is a form of internal knowledge, which usually shows up as our first impression. It is a gift from spirit, the small inner voice that suggests courses of action that need to be taken. Many think of intuition as a gut feeling or a hunch. Sometimes the information is unexpected, so we may tend to think that it is invalid.

   Our intellect may encourage us to deny this spiritual knowing by telling us "This doesn't make sense." However, it is important to our spiritual growth, and our well being, that we acknowledge these feelings and act upon them. Many times these intuitive feelings may seem illogical or out of step with our conscious mind, thought processes, or what we consider "reality." We may be reluctant to follow it. We should become still, listen, and follow through on what we receive. The more we use our intuition, the sharper it becomes. As a result, we will have a more successful and fulfilling life and be better able to avoid negative circumstances. The next time you hear that inner voice, follow it!

7. **WRITE IT OUT** – As students, we frequently had to write compositions, poems, and term papers. We may or may not have felt good about these writing assignments, but they were, nonetheless, required. Aside from being an educational requirement, writing, or journaling, can be used for our personal benefit. This occurs when we use writing as a vehicle through which we can relieve stress and get to know our inner selves. When issues confront us, we can write down our feelings about these issues. This activity helps us in getting to the bottom of what happened and how we feel about it, and helps prevent us from turning emotional hurts and challenges into physical disease.

It is helpful to purchase a journal that is solely dedicated to capturing your experiences on a regular and consistent basis. Looking back on our journals allows us to monitor our spiritual and emotional growth, and to identify areas of our lives that need more work. Writing down our dreams, once we awaken, enables us to review our subconscious beliefs and feelings. If we are experiencing a specific problem, we may want to quiet ourselves, ask for God's guidance, meditate and begin to write whatever comes to mind. This practice allows whatever information we need to know to float up from the recesses of our beings into the light of our conscious minds.

8. **OVERCOME FEAR** – Many of us have had great ideas and great plans for things that we want to accomplish, but for some reason we got stuck at the idea or planning stage never to realize our dreams. Fear is one of the reasons that we do not follow through to accomplish our plans, dreams, or goals. As a result, we have not offered these gifts to the universe. Even as mature adults, we are sometimes fearful of taking on new direction or a new path. Sometimes the fear is conscious (whereby we know what we are afraid of), and at times it may be unconscious. Some of the common fears that prevent some of us from moving ahead include: others' disapproval, failure, lack of resources, or the unknown. However, fear blocks our potential, our prosperity, and our growth.

   We all have our individual talents and gifts we can offer to one another, and this offering puts us in flow with the universe and ensures that our prosperity and growth will continue. As we increase our faith in God, we realize that our lives are always in Divine Order. We can step out and take chances based upon the faith that God is always here. Remember that we are beings of love and light and where there is love and light, fear dissipates.

9. **GET AN EARLIER START ON THE DAY** – Many times we feel as though we never have enough time for ourselves—or to engage in our favorite hobbies, rituals, or personal pampering. When we feel deprived, our spirits can become bogged down and slightly depressed. We can have more time for ourselves and alleviate these "deprived" feelings by rising earlier in the day. Getting up earlier, when the day is new and the air is fresh, can enable us to have time to do any number of things that feed our spirits. I *know*. We get so exhausted from all of the activities that we feel we must do, how can we possibly get up any earlier? Well, we *can*. Maybe at first we will groggily awaken to the sound of an alarm clock, but it will be worth it.

     Throughout my life, I frequently wished that I had more time to read, exercise, pray, sew, or reflect, among many other things. I found that early mornings are the perfect time for these activities. When I experienced a yearning for these things, I have gotten up earlier to meditate, read, indulge in my favorite hobby, dress leisurely, or just relax. The result has been that I have found more joy in living my life. Although it may initially seem to you that missing an hour of sleep will be devastating, actually you will be leading a more fulfilling life that will provide you with more energy than you could imagine.

10. **TAKE CHARGE OF YOUR LIFE'S DRAMA** – Each of our personal lives can be likened to a play or drama. In this play we are the writers, producers, directors, and the main characters. If we do not like what is happening in this play, or we want to change our lives, we have the power to alter the storyline, setting, props, and the characters, including ourselves. We can go within ourselves and shine the spotlight into the corners of our lives. Once the lights are on, it may take courage to accept what we are seeing.

However, this acceptance is the first step to changing the undesirable elements of our lives.

We should not be afraid to question our roles or the dialogue in our play. Sometimes we tend to overly focus on the idea that the other characters in our play are the source of our life's problems and believe these people to be more powerful than they actually are. Really, they are only actors in *our* play, acting as best they can with the training they have. It is our responsibility to change the script and/or characters as needed.

The work we must do requires stillness, spending some time alone, prayer, meditation, listening, and sometimes seeking outside counsel. Once we acquire insight, we must use our strength and power to make the proper changes. If we find that the circumstances or our lives are out of control, or that events in our lives are not going as we would have them, we should step back a little, review the development of our play, and make the necessary edits. Remember, we can change the plot, the scenery, or the characters, if necessary.

11. **PONDER THE POSITIVE** – It is hard to ignore all of the negative news and information that takes up so much time and space in our lives. For me, the negative items seem to grab my attention, and even when seemingly dismissed, have left their footprints somewhere in my consciousness. Of course, as people are disturbed by negative events, they tend to repeatedly discuss them. I find it easy to get caught up in the unrelenting stories of negative occurrences in the world and in my personal community.

On the other hand, there are so many positive things going on each and every day. I remind myself that these are the blessings that should more frequently grab my attention. The greatest blessing we all have is to be alive! Each day there are so many unnoticed miracles and blessings that continue to come to us. These things should be pondered and appreciated. Try this: the next time you are bombarded with negative experiences, images, or thoughts, replace them with positive thoughts. Although this practice may seem challenging at first, we *can* control our thoughts. The more this is done, the more we will fill our days with positive thoughts, feelings, and occurrences. In the end, together we can create a more positive world.

12. **LIVE IN THE PRESENT MOMENT** – We live in a world where everyday happenings from around the entire world are continuously reported to us through the media. It seems that most of these reported events have the ability to create fear, anxiety, worry, and apprehension in the general populace. One of the ways to combat anxiety is to live in the present moment. If we can become conscious and aware of what is happening with us right now, at this very moment, we will find that all is well.

Someone once wrote that the present is called the "present" because it is a gift. If we feel our thoughts and fears running away with us, we can say, " "STOP," take a few deep abdominal breaths, sense our bodies and spirits, and know that we are doing and being well. We cannot change the past or control exactly what happens in the future. But, this very moment is precious, and all is well.

13. **REMEMBER THAT GOD IS ALWAYS WITH US** – No matter where we are, or where we go, we are never alone because the spirit of God is always with us. Whether we are going through frustrating situations during our work day, or whether we are experiencing challenges in trying to guide our children on a positive life path, we always have the strength of the Creator right here with us at all times. Know this: we have no need to feel anxiety about out present circumstances, or to fear what may happen to us in the future. There is no need for us to worry about our travels

away from home or our experiences at home, as the spirit of God lives within us wherever we may be.

If we should ever become disturbed by the events or the condition of our lives, we can take time to visualize God's light around and through us. In the glow of that light, know that at the very moment, we are protected and all is well. We are so loved by God!

14. **LISTEN TO OUR CHILDREN** – Many times in writing, I refer to things that my grandchildren have said or done to serve as examples of lessons that I have learned or truths that I believe. I really believe that young people, no matter how young, have much to teach us, and that it is a blessing to be able to watch and hear them. Oftentimes, although they may be young in birth years, they are mature in spirit.

Children also have clarity and they observe things that we tend to overlook because of our preoccupation with life events. If we talk with them, we find that they are more straightforward and honest in their statements. They have not yet learned to say what is "appropriate" or what people just want to hear. When they come to us with something to say, we should stop and take the time to really hear them. They could be delivering a message from God.

15. **PRAY FOR LOVED ONES** – All of us have people in our lives that we love and want to help. The best way to help them is to pray for them in a constant manner. When we pray for them, we are energetically surrounding them with light and love. Whatever challenges they are facing will be lessened through the gift of prayer.

Personally, I have experienced that whenever I have been away from and missed people that I love, I have actually been able to feel a closer connection to them by praying for them. I know that those we love cannot help but feel the warmth of our love when we pray for them. Even when we are unable to determine or provide for their needs in the physical realm, our prayers for their highest good in all things will cover all of the areas in which they have need.

16. **STAY IN FLOW WITH THE WEATHER** –For all of the mild hysteria that we feel in the Mid-Atlantic region once the media predicts snow, the arrival of the snow is quietly graceful. Although snow leaves the environment more beautiful than before its arrival, it does bring with it the possibility of inconvenience and danger. One snowy morning in January, I was impressed by how silently and serenely the vast fluffy mounds of snow were coming into form.

Just watching the snowfall seemed to lull me into a meditative state, and I began to internalize the quiet and the peace that the snow brings. It was so quiet, so divinely quiet. I began to think that it is rather sad that the forecast of snow makes people so nervous and anxious. Rather than concentrating on the beauty that nature has provided us, we are more concerned with how we may be inconvenienced and prevented from moving on with whatever plans we have. Instead of feeling dismayed or confined, we would feel much better going with the flow of nature. Snowy days are a perfect time to slow down, because nature is slowing us down. We are given an opportunity to catch our breath, do some inner work, and perhaps spend more time with our families. It is a perfect time to be grateful for having a warm, secure place in which to live.

When we cultivate an attitude of nonresistance toward the weather, we can adapt ourselves to the changing seasons with cheerfulness. Rain, snow, wind, thunderstorms, as well as sunshine, are expressions of the Divine.

17. **CHOOSE TO HAVE QUIET TIMES** – On one of my travels to Philadelphia, I decided to travel by Amtrak train instead of driving there. As I walked along the platform, I heard the conductor say, "Quiet car right here; regular cars ahead." I saw people walking past this quiet car, but a small elderly woman boarded the car. I stopped and asked the conductor to define "quiet," and he said, "No cell phones and no loud conversations." I was intrigued and decided to try the quiet car. It was amazing to me how many people just passed by the quiet car and did not even attempt to board it.

It seems that people today are adverse to quiet. On a fifty-seat quiet car going from Washington to Boston, there were only five people in the quiet car. This car was so beautiful, so peaceful, and meticulously clean. I began to think that as we quiet our lives in general, the benefits of beauty, peace, and orderliness are frequently our rewards. Taking special time for ourselves, and experiencing some quiet, is essential to our well being. When choosing to spend more time alone, we may not be aware of all of the ins, outs, and dramas of everyday life and what the majority of our associates are doing. However, in turn, we achieve more peace, beauty, and clarity in our lives. This can only be a good thing.

18. **LAUGH** – Laughter is one of the best ways to reduce stress, and studies have suggested that laughter may also boost immunity, relieve pain, lower blood sugar in people with Type 2 diabetes, and help protect against heart disease. And, if these benefits are not enough for you, the American Association for Therapeutic Humor says that a good laugh changes blood pressure, reduces muscle tension, improves digestion, and increases alertness. The medical community is increasingly studying the effects that positive emotions have on our health and well being.

How can we add more laughter to our lives and brighten our mood? We can read humorous books, articles, or cartoons. We can try looking around our world to find the humor in everyday occurrences. If we keep our eyes open, we will easily see humorous things happening daily. If we do not find enough funny material in our environment, we can try watching comedies in theaters, on DVDs, or on television. Spend some time with a friend who makes you laugh. For me, spending time with the friends that enable me to laugh results in my feeling cleansed, clearer, and uplifted. Additionally, we should be able to look at ourselves and find humor in some of our own responses to life's issues. Remember to share your laughter with others.

19. **ALWAYS TAKE THE HIGH ROAD** – In life, we have many paths and courses of action from which to choose, especially when we are confronted with challenges. These paths may be separated into two categories: the high road and the low road. Always choose the high road.

Oftentimes, the low road seems very familiar. We know the markers, the convenience stops, and the scenery. We feel comfortable moving along this road. There may be fewer challenges to confront, and usually we are allowed to continue the behavior with which we identify ourselves. We know many of the fellow travelers, and we are in step with them. We may be allowed to move at a slower pace on this road.

The high road may be challenging, but we will learn new things about others and about ourselves. On the high road, we may have to suspend judgment, criticism, or argumentation but we will achieve growth, wisdom, and peace. On the high road we observe what is happening and if someone does something against us, we pray and contemplate what to do rather than engage in immediate retaliation.

Letting go of outmoded beliefs and situations releases blockages in our energy field and allows us to manifest experiences that enhance our growth. The high road may be steep and require a different level of energy, but in the end the rewards for taking this road are immeasurable. Ultimately, we will find that we are closer to living the perfection that our lives are meant to be.

20. **MAKE TIME FOR MEDITATION** – We all have busy schedules, and it seems that the longer we live, the more projects we find ourselves involved in. Sometimes we are under time constraints whereby we have so many responsibilities to take care of within a small period of time. There is an inclination to get the most out of every minute in order to fit more activities into our schedules than we can even complete.

It is at these very times that we may lean toward skipping our meditation time, and/or to shorten the length of our meditation and prayers. Sometimes we may be too fatigued from all of our daily activities to concentrate during meditation and prayer times. It is precisely at these times of stress that we should increase our meditation time. The best way to deal with the stress of daily living is to periodically take time out to become still and contact the God that is within all of us. We then find that ultimately we have more time because we are performing our activities from a place of peace and with the assistance and power of God.

21. **TELL IT TO THE APPROPRIATE PERSON** – We sometimes have disagreements with the people who are in our lives. Perhaps we feel that someone has disrespected us or done us some harm or injustice. It is common to mull these situations over in our minds and then tell a friend or family member about the problem we are experiencing.

Once we have talked about our issue to that caring person who listens to us, that may be all that is necessary. However, there are times when we need to tell the "appropriate person," that is, the person with whom we are at odds. After talking to our confidants and getting their ideas, we may need to contact the appropriate person and begin a heart-to-heart dialogue about the issue or problem at hand.

I am not suggesting that we stop confiding in our friends. I am telling you that in order to stay emotionally healthy and centered, and also physically healthy, we may need to go one more step. We may be emotionally overwrought, and find it difficult to confront this person. Nevertheless, if we find a way to talk to the appropriate person, with an open heart, there will be less emotional baggage for us to haul around and our lives will be lighter and happier.

22. **DO ONE THING AT A TIME** – Many of us ambitiously try to maximize the use of the twenty-four hours that we are allotted each day. We want to accomplish so much. In so doing, we have often gotten into the habit of doing many things at one time. We have found that we can eat lunch, cook dinner, talk on the phone, and sort our laundry *all at the same time*. However, we frequently find that we have indigestion, have burned the food, not understood anything the person on the other end of the phone has said, and put two mismatched socks together! I have made each of these mistakes.

Being inefficient is just one result of doing many tasks at once. More importantly, during the "multi-tasking", we are unable to adequately find enjoyment in any of the things we are doing. We are not living in the present moment, and that is where our peace lies. I struggle to enforce doing one thing at a time in my own life. For example, I have made a conscious effort to eat and *do nothing*. I find that eating then becomes a form of meditation. I can better taste the food, sense its texture, and be consciously grateful for the contribution it makes to my health. I do not feel this way when I am attempting to do other tasks while eating.

Paying attention to what I am doing allows me to see God in whatever I am experiencing. I find that I am happier doing whatever I am doing – and I am doing it well. The result is more focused, peaceful living.

23. **BECOME A SOURCE OF LOVE** – The month of February is the month of Valentine's Day, and it is this month that society has assigned a "day" for love. Many people spend much of their lives looking for love from others. They look at other people's relationships and wish they were receiving the amount of love from their husband/wife, children, friends, family, as they perceive others are receiving – or maybe just an amount that they feel they deserve.

When we feel we need more love in our lives, the best thing we can do is become love. As we begin to feel and display more love to those around us, we find that love is returned to us. I am not necessarily referring to romantic love. Start to feel as much love in your life as possible: love your family, friends, co-workers, and your environment in general. Start doing loving things. Love is energy like everything else, and when we put it out there, it is returned to us. Don't forget to send some love to yourself, as well.

In time, we will begin to see more and more love showing up in our lives as we give more and more. And by the way, let's make every day of our lives a day of love. We know that we do not have to wait until February 14.

24. **BLESS YOUR FOOD** – Most of us were taught, as children, to say a blessing or prayer over our food before eating. From childhood through adulthood, I thought of "saying grace" as a way of thanking God for the food I had to eat, especially

since a vast number of the world's population goes to bed hungry. Most of us are still blessing our food, as well we should.

However, in recent years, I have begun to not only express gratitude for the food, but also to ask God to infuse the food with light and health-enhancing properties. This is especially important these days when produce is sometimes lacking its life-giving properties and may have traces of pesticides, chemicals, and toxins. Meats frequently contain antibiotics, hormones, or growth-promoting substances – all of which may have adverse effects on our systems. We should send blessings to those who cultivate and prepare the food we eat. If we eat animals, we should thank these animals for offering their lives and bodies for our nourishment.

Some people feel self-conscious about blessing their food when they are eating in restaurants or public places. This is an especially good time to pause, and quietly say a blessing. We are fortunate enough to have the financial resources to eat out. On the other hand, we did not prepare this food ourselves. We should invoke the presence of God in all food, so that it will nourish our bodies in the way that God intended.

25. **BLESS AND RESPECT ANIMALS** – I have known several people who have had car accidents that involved animals. As each person related how their particular accident occurred, I heard how disturbed and anguished they were and how they prayed that the hurt animal would not die. At that moment, they felt the connection with the pain of the animal. On the other hand, I think of my friends that have pets that they live with and care for every day, and I am reminded of the loving connection that they have to their animals. Although completely different situations, they touched me because of the feeling and responsibility each person felt for God's

creatures. We do have a responsibility to the animals to show them love and to protect them as much as possible.

As humans, we are constantly taking more and more of the animals' habitat for ourselves. Many of them are displaced and are wandering dangerously around our neighborhoods, which were once the animals' living space. As we see them or walk along their paths, we should bless them for their presence and purpose here. Even if we make small gestures, such as placing bird feed on our property, we are helping the animals and enhancing our connection with nature. Those who have animals as pets, and care for them daily, are expressing God's love for an essential part of creation. And, in turn, the animals give much love back to their caretakers. All animals have intelligence and teach us so much just by their very existence. They are truly a blessing to us all.

26. **AVOID NEGATIVE THOUGHTS AND CONVERSATIONS** – Many of us are traveling a spiritual path in our lives and have made magnificent strides in our spiritual growth. It is sometimes disconcerting, when it appears that *all of a sudden* we are having negative experiences. Of course, the definition of a "positive" or "negative" experience is subjective and personal to each of us as individuals. But, for example, some of us have experienced a loss of a job, health, finances, friends, or peace of mind. Although these losses can have positive lessons and outcomes down the line, we may experience suffering in the present moment.

As we move to higher spiritual levels, we are held accountable for the wisdom and knowledge we have attained. As a result, when we engage in negative thoughts, actions, conversations, and criticism, we see the results of this negativity in our physical, mental, or emotional bodies. From my personal experience, the results of these negative actions occur more quickly at this particular time on the planet than occurred in the past. We are sometimes left sitting and wondering, "What happened?" I believe that if we look at any negative "situation" we are experiencing right now, we can trace it to some negative thought pattern or negative speech. Therefore, we can all benefit from trying to keep our thoughts clear, true, and positive. We must start by affirming only the positive in our lives. However, if we fall back into a negative thought pattern, we must stop immediately and affirm the good that we know is always present. In this way, we can keep our minds and bodies in perfect Divine Order and be the lights to the world that we truly are.

27. **FORGIVE YOURSELF FOR YOUR MISTAKES** – Sometime we say or do things that we are not especially proud of and later tend to regret. When we make what we consider "mistakes," we sometimes may replay the situation in question over and over again in our minds. We may even develop guilt feelings about our actions.

Whether or not our behavior was correct or incorrect, it is necessary to forgive ourselves and move on. It is helpful to prayerfully review our actions and determine what may have gone wrong, but we need not get stuck there. As we forgive others for their actions, we must be kind enough to do the same for ourselves. If we have hurt other people, we should ask them for forgiveness and know that God forgives us.

If we find that we are still haunted by our actions and have not moved forward or let go, perhaps we need to take steps to treat ourselves lovingly. We can pray more, get more rest, or go outside and commune with nature, and not hold ourselves by a harsher standard than we hold others. Take time apart to slow down, be still, and reflect. We are spiritual beings and it is helpful to ask God for peace and tranquility—and affirm and visualize this peace and tranquility within and around ourselves. There is never a time when we are not living in the heart of God. When we continue to discredit and criticize ourselves, we forget our importance to the Universe and to God. God loves us and forgives us. To really love ourselves we must begin to see ourselves as God sees us.

28. **BE GRATEFUL FOR THE POSITIVE THINGS IN LIFE** –We are surrounded by positive situations at all times. Always! We only have to *see* them. There are not enough reports about the good things that are going on in our communities.

However, we should take the time to look around us and see the good that others are doing. Every day, I see people supporting one another in a myriad of ways, and this is uplifting. We can also remind ourselves of the good that is occurring in our own lives. These blessings should be at the forefront of our minds rather than the proliferation of negative images and ideas that are so commonplace in our lives. We should always be grateful for these blessings. Our greatest blessing is having life—as this life affords us the opportunity to see, and participate in, all of the miracles and wonderful things that happen daily.

The more we express gratitude for our blessings—our health, our lives, and our prosperity—the less we will concentrate on the negative happenings in our communities. As we are thankful, we begin to see more blessings. We become happier, less stressed, and by showing gratitude, we make the way for our blessings to increase.

29. **GO OUT ALONE** – We have all experienced a time when we excitedly asked friends or family members to accompany us on a particular outing. After making several telephone calls, we found that no one was available to go. This has

happened to me on several occasions, and sometimes, because I did not want to venture out alone, I missed out on what I wanted to do. Maybe I missed a museum exhibit, a dinner at a new, exotic restaurant, or just sitting on the beach.

However, on the occasions when I decided that I would go out alone, I had a great time! Once at my destination, I may have had the opportunity to make new acquaintances, or conversely I may have spoken to no one. Either way, the experience was good, and I felt elated about having treated myself to something that I wanted to do.

We really are our own best friends, and at every moment in life we have an opportunity to learn and experience something new through our own eyes. If we cannot find a companion to share experiences with, we can eventually share the details and feelings about the experience with our friends later on. When we say "yes" to opportunities and experiences that we find delightful, we prove to ourselves that we are worthy and deserving of our own time and attention. We deserve the best.

30. **ENCOURAGE OTHERS** – When I was a child, I was fortunate enough to have parents and grandparents who continually encouraged me to succeed in whatever I attempted to do. If I had difficulty accomplishing some project, they would always tell me that I could accomplish *anything*. They helped me and would not allow me to give up. Whether I made good grades in school or made a dress for my doll out of fabric scraps, one of them seemed to always tell me what a good job I had done.

Many of you probably had similar childhood experiences and gave that type of support and encouragement to your children or other children. But what happens when we become adults? As adults, we still need encouragement to be the best we can be while we continually undertake life's challenges. As part of the human family, we have a responsibility to encourage one another. As we see those around us striving to accomplish their goals, or maybe just trying to maintain their strength and sanity while dealing with everyday responsibilities, we can offer them kind words of encouragement and support. Telling them what a good job they have done in some particular area, or compassionately offering them suggestions on how to get through whatever they are facing, are excellent ways to provide encouragement.

Your words of encouragement can help boost the spirits of those around you, and may serve as the impetus for them to persevere and move more easily along their paths. No matter what chronological age we may have achieved, there is still a child within each of us that smiles and pushes forward when given approval and support.

Affirmations

There are times when we want to achieve a positive state of consciousness, or positive outcome, in a particular aspect or our lives. Positive affirmations are a fantastic aid in achieving whatever we want to show up in our lives.

Affirmations are positive statements about some condition or circumstance. In speaking affirmations, we are saying that some condition is true, even if there appears to be evidence to the contrary. In essence, we are speaking the ultimate truth about ourselves, or about our situations. By repeating affirmations, we lead our minds to a place where the mind accepts as true that which the heart *knows* and the mind wants to believe. Words are very powerful and form the basis for the reality we experience. By knowing and stating the truth about ourselves, we find that we begin to embody that truth.

In the section below, I have listed thirty affirmations that I wrote to relate to specific life conditions or states of consciousness that you may want to achieve. Ideally, I suggest that you say a prayer, silently read the affirmation, let the meaning or the affirmation permeate your being, and then say the affirmation out loud. Repeat the affirmation as many times as possible during the day.

If you need immediate help, or are pressed for time, you can just say the affirmation whenever you feel the need, silently (within your being) or out loud, without going through the steps I mentioned above. Whichever way you say the affirmations, it is crucial to know that the desired outcome has been achieved, as God loves you and wants only the best for you. At the end of affirming your truth, be sure to say "thank you" to God.

1. **Love**
   I am continuously experiencing loving relationships and situations in my life. God loves me.

2. **Peace**
   Increasingly aware of God's presence, I am total peace.

3. **Health**
   The healing power of God infuses perfection in every cell of my body, my mind, and my spirit. I am perfect health!

4. **Prosperity/Abundance**
   God's universe has unlimited supply. I am claiming my unlimited prosperity right now.

5. **Faith**
   God supports me in all that I do. I am one with God and all is well.

6. **Protection**
   I am protected by God's love at all times, in all places. Divine Protection is mine.

7. **Letting Go**
   I now let go and let God be God, the ultimate Force, in my life. I willingly turn this situation over to God.

8. **Patience**
I am steadfastly patient in all things knowing that God is bringing forth my highest good.

9. **Relaxation**
I am letting go of all that causes me stress, and I experience perfect calm.

10. **Divine Order**
Like the perfect order of nature, Divine Order is continually restored in my life and all of my affairs.

11. **Fearlessness**
The love of God casts out all fear, and I follow my path unafraid.

12. **Gratitude**
I am so grateful for all of the gifts in my life, especially the gift of life itself.

13. **Relationships**
My relationships are infused with the love of God. I see God in all people.

14. **Worry-free**
With God in charge, I am confident of my eternal good and I am free of all worries.

15. **Giving**
I give freely with the total awareness that I have plenty, and as I give I also receive.

16. **Guidance**

   I ask for, and follow, the wisdom of God. God guides me toward right action.

17. **Transformation**

   Every day, in every way, I am becoming better and better.

18. **Joy**

   Joy and happiness fill my life every minute of the day. I choose to be joyful, and happiness radiates from my entire being.

19. **World Peace**

   With peace in my heart, I bless the entire Earth with peace and loving thoughts.

20. **Creativity**

   With the influx of Divine ideas and Divine inspiration, I create only that which is good.

21. **Responsibility**

   With God's help, I recognize and accept all for which I am responsible, and I accomplish great things.

22. **Harmony**

   I ask God how to live in harmony with all things. I am lovingly connected to all that is around me.

23. **Comfort**

   The Holy Spirit of God gently caresses and comforts me, and I feel good.

24. **Prayer for Others**

Precious one, God is blessing you with peace, health, love, prosperity, and joy right now and always.

25. **Strength**

As God is my strength, I remain strong through all of life's challenges.

26. **Self-Worth**

Being a beloved child of God, the Creator, I love and appreciate myself.

27. **Being Alone**

Since God is my constant Companion and Friend, I am never alone.

28. **Stillness/Quiet**

Through my stillness, as I choose to be quiet, I am continually hearing the voice of God. Be still, and know, that I am God.

29. **Forgiveness**

As God always forgives me, I forgive all others and my life is positively transformed.

30. **Will**

I will only that which is the will of God. I am one with the will of God.

Epilogue

I am very grateful for your purchasing and reading this book. I hope that some of the material I offer touched you in a positive manner, and that it will help you while you travel your spiritual journey. My desire is that the book will help many to move forward in an easier, more joyful manner and that their paths will be smoother.

In closing, I want to remind you that we are surrounded by many fellow spiritual travelers who are also seeking higher truths and ways to live more rewarding and fulfilling lives. They, too, desire to make a positive difference as they face life's joys and challenges. Once you have begun your journey in earnest, just look around, and you will recognize them. Acknowledge these fellow travelers with a smile and, when needed, a helping hand. In this way, we provide support for each other and as our paths intertwine, all of our journeys become full of light and love.

Selected Reading

Bruyere, Rosalyn L. *Wheels of Light*. Fireside, 1994.

Chopra, Deepak. *The Seven Spiritual Laws of Success*. Amber Allen Publishing, 1994.

Dossey, Larry. *Prayer is Good Medicine*. Harper Collins, 1996.

Dyer, Wayne W. *Manifest Your Destiny*. Harper Collins, 1917.

Dyer, Wayne W. *Your Sacred Self*. Harper Paperbacks, 1995.

Filmore, Charles. *Jesus Christ Heals*. Unity Books, 1999.

Hasbrouck, Hypatia. *Handbook of Positive Prayer*. Unity House, 2004.

Hay, Louise L. *You Can Heal Your Life*. Hay House, 1987.

Holmes, Ernest. *Prayer*. Tarcher/Penguin, 2008.

Holmes, Ernest. *The Science of Mind*. Penguin Putnam, 1998.

Keville, Kathi and Mindy Green. *Aromatherapy: A Complete Guide to the Healing Art*. The Crossing Press, 1995.

Peale, Norman Vincent. *The Power of Positive Thinking*. Prentice-Hall, Inc.,1952.

Simpson, Liz. *The Book of Chakra Healing*. Sterling Publishing Company. 1999.

Worwood, Valerie Ann. *The Complete Book Of Essential Oils and Aromatherapy*, New World Library, 1991.

About the Author

Susan Duncan writes the "Living In The Light" newsletter, and she has appeared on radio programs and led seminars to encourage spiritual growth and natural healing. She designs and sells jewelry through her company, Crystalight Designs. A graduate of Howard University, she lives in the Washington, D.C. suburbs.